The Lil' Author Skool presents

Daydreamers

edited by Abiola Bello

By Various Authors

Published in Great Britain by Hashtag Press 2022

HashtagPRESS

HASHTAG PRESS BOOKS
Hashtag Press Ltd
Kent, England, United Kingdom
Email: info@hashtagpress.co.uk
Website: www.hashtagpress.co.uk
Twitter: @hashtag_press

Acknowledgements

When lockdown happened I wasn't sure when the third book from young writers would happen but I was pleased and impressed when so many entries came in despite the pandemic. I thought Daydreamers was the perfect title to sum up this book. Lockdown really did give us all enough time to daydream!

All of these young writers are brilliant and I want to thank each of you for writing such a great story. I know you will be a bestseller someday.

Much love to Hashtag Press for sponsoring Daydreamers and investing 50% of the production costs and Helen Braid for bringing my dreamy cover to life.

Daydreamers is the third book from The Lil' Author Skool and as always the talent doesn't disappoint. I hope these stories encourage, entertain and transport you.

Abiola
Founder of The Lil' Author Skool

For the latest news, info on The little BIG Book Comp and exclusive materials from The Lil' Author Skool visit:

www.thelilauthorskool.com
or connect with us on:
Twitter @LilAuthorSkool
Instagram @thelilauthorskool
Facebook.com/thelilauthorskool

To every young person who dares to dream

Winners' Stories

A Memoir in Ice

By Atlas Weyland Eden
Fourteen years old from Devon, England

I was born on a tiny island in the middle of the Baltic Sea. Of course, it wasn't the Baltic Sea back then, but an endless ocean of shadow and ice. If you asked me to point on a map to where I was born, I shall point there.

My father was Frost and my mother was Snow. This was before the first dragons were born and the plates beneath the earth began to shift. There were stars yet to be conceived.

Alone? No, we were far from alone. There were bears on the island. My parents gave me to them when I was a few days old. They knew the bears would educate me in all the ways I would need.

My early years were spent in deep caves beneath tangled forests. I curled with the cubs, suckled from the breast of Mother Bear. My first speech was the prickle of ice and rain, but my favourite tongue will always be the growling hymns of bears.

When I was grown enough to hunt food, the first great change came upon my life. A storm brewed in the sky, the first of the great storms which ravished the world. It was one night that a shaft of lightning felled a tree. The sound woke me from my bearskin dreams. The others moaned in fear, but I ventured on all fours to the fallen tree.

I still have that first carving. I keep it in my desk. It's of rough black wood, a type long extinct today. I suppose I meant it to be a bear, though I was less skilled then. The bears recognised the potential in my early art. Knowing they could not teach me such things, they sent me to train with the white woodpeckers, to learn the ways of whittling.

A woodpecker is a wicked teacher. They are the greatest of perfectionists, and my skill only accentuated this. I still have the scars where they pecked my hands when I whittled something wrong. One carving I did with uneven eyes, and they opened the veins between my thumb and my wrist but I would not miss those lessons for anything in the world. I became the greatest of carvers, until the eldest woodpeckers bowed their beaks in defeat.

The day I graduated from their teachings, I resolved to leave the island. I was young and had visions of adventure. With my bear-sharp claws I brought down a tree, with my woodpecker-skill I turned it into a boat.

My parents came to wish me goodbye. My father gave me his second-best knife, my mother gave me her birch-bark paints. I set sail from the stony coast, delving into mists, which hung above the sea.

Land? I knew of none. The continents were unformed; mountains lay beneath waves. The only map I had were the stars in the sky and the songs in my mind. I sailed for a long time, living on mist and moonlight, until I moored on an utterly frozen land. This was nothing like my island: as soon I stepped on its surface I felt its size, stretching beyond the horizon and into the sky. It would be where Russia is now, though back then we knew it only as North.

I left my boat on the shore and waded through snow. I stayed a while in this land. I passed through villages, earning wonder and respect for the carvings I made. In time I built a hold for myself: my own hall made with my own hands. I gained followers, gnomes and wood sprites; black beasts who came to my hall to sit by my heels.

Will it surprise you to hear I was a warring god? I was young and strong, with hands that could break as well as make. When I looked from my hall, I saw a wide unconquered land and wished it to be mine. I battled giants who had laid claim to it, I pillaged towns and slaughtered babes. I rode before armies, drank honeyed mead from my enemies' skulls.

I heard tales of The Glacier King, a monarch reining in the frozen east. I went to him, sat at his table and ate his meats. His daughter sat by his side. She wore a gown of stars, her face as delicate as falling snow. She danced for us after the feast, her skirt twirling like a song.

I wanted her. I told as much to her father: I offered my knife and my paints as a dowry, but he refused. I marched my army to his palace and broke upon his door. I found him in the throne room and cracked his head on the floor. I hung his lungs about my neck. I carried his daughter from her chambers and we were wed in my hall.

We were happy together. We still are. I gave her everything she asked for: I believe she gave me more. As the nights went by, love softened my hand and I wearied of war. My armies fell apart. My wife and I took to walking the ice-fields together, watching mammoths graze.

My life changed again with the first sunrise. The world was lit only by moon and stars, but spring had begun. The snows thawed and the land turned green. Birds trilled and flowers waved in bloom. But my wife and I are creatures of winter, and we missed the cool nights. We left the hall and migrated north. We crossed seas and mountain ranges newly born. We spent our evenings in a tent, huddled close as the day's fire smoked and died.

We arrived at the very top of the world. Here, at the most northerly point, the ice was still fresh and the glaciers floated free. We set a pole in the earth to mark our home: no wind has ever knocked it down.

We built, not a hall, but a humble cottage, from the pines that clustered in the cold. It was there—here—that I focused again on my work. War had made me sloppy, so I refined my art in the woodpecker way. My wife practised pastry, though she never told me where she got the wheat. They are my fondest memories: a pie sizzling by the hearth, the snow a-thunder outside, while I finished a sculpture from the leg of an old chair.

One morning I strode outside, my cloak wrapped about me to watch the sunset. The days are short and brilliant here, sunrise only slightly preceding sunset. As the snow glowed scarlet-pink, I felt a susurrus in the earth. I lowered my ear and heard footsteps under the ice. I struck my staff against the snow. It broke into crystals, revealing a cave. I saw a gathering of creatures, small sprightly beings: a colony of ice elves. They gazed at me with wonder, each the height of a child. I helped them out and resealed the hole. I learned they were tunnelling underground, fleeing a thaw in the

West, when the cave collapsed around them, leaving them trapped.

We took them in and wrapped them in blankets and sat them by the fire. They whispered with each other, while I whittled a bear. Their eyes followed my hands, widening as my creation came to completion. Later, a chosen representative approached me. He stood, eyes fixed on his feet. At last, he asked me to teach them to carve.

They were good students. Woodwork came naturally to them, though they were perfectionists of a kind I had not seen since the white woodpeckers. When they honed their skill to a place that pleased them, they produced with greater force. Every day, dozens of sculptures were churned out. They filled the shelves, the cupboards, jostling for room. We grew fond of the elves: we built them a cottage for they had no wish to leave, but there was no room for their carvings.

The first traces of the idea came to me. I was in bed with my wife, mulling it over with a good wine. It would be a commitment, something to keep me busy through the long night but what else did I have to do here in the farthest north?

I sent the message with the birds, to every household they could find. A song for the ears of children:

> *Write a letter: name all the toys you wish.*
> *Send it north, and hang a stocking*
> *on the longest night of the year.*

The letters came thick and fast. They asked for all manner of things, plenty the elves had already made, and some we never imagined. I took out my birch-bark paints, sharpened my knife, and we set to work sculpting their dreams.

Leading up to the main event, I wondered how to get around the world in one night. I heard a rumour of a reindeer as old as Orion, who could fly the sky like a bird. I found her grazing on a frosty outcrop, her four antlers framing the night. Oh, how I loved that beast. She thrashed beneath my weight, bucked with all her might. I held tight to her coat, as her antlers tore my cheek. We rolled together in blood and snow, her hair in my mouth. We cartwheeled through the northern lights. She relented and admitted I was worthy. I fashioned a sleigh from timber; she accepted the harness, watching the elves load presents.

On the darkest night, she pulled the sleigh into the sky. In my experience, time is fickle and easily changed: midnight had scarcely tolled when we filled the last of the stockings. A victory feast was held when we arrived home: lamb and hog and several geese. When we finished, the ravaged bones reformed themselves and the geese flew away.

My wife kissed me. She thought me mad—she still does. Delivering elf-made gifts to every child under the moon? It is certainly mad. That is why I do it.

It was Boxing Day, when the reindeer fell into the snow. Her belly writhed. She bit my hand when I came close, but there was farewell in her teeth. Her time had come. As she closed her eyes, eight lumps of fur fell from between her legs. They sniffed the air before stumbling to their hoofs. They nibbled my fingers, half-blind. I picked them up and put them by the fire. I went for milk; when I returned, one was prancing through the air.

They were all boys, each as proud as their mother. There were only eight then. The ninth came later—but that is another story. The reindeer grew quickly. They were big enough to tow the sleigh by the next moon. They are smaller than their mother: it takes all eight to drag me into the sky.

Little has changed since then. I am older now. I leave most of the carving to the elves these days—my hands are not what they once were—but I make my mad ride into the night. I mount the sleigh, harness the reindeer, and soar through all the world.

Hmm? Am I leaving things untold? You are right, most likely. I have lived a long time, seen many things, heard countless tales but what good is life without mysteries? Without stories you will never know?

I have talked long enough for one night. The moon is high, the elves are working, and somewhere bears sing. Why don't you stay for tea? My wife is baking mince pies.

Storm Song

By Nicky Anderson
Fifteen years old from Cumbria, England

My favourite colour is Ocean Blue, which is lucky, since I've been surrounded by lapping waves my entire life. My favourite smell is baking bread, which I make every Sunday, rain or shine, without fail. The smell reminds me of my mother, and the hours she would spend in the kitchen; brewing, boiling, and baking her worries away. My favourite memory is of three years ago, the night of July the fifth, when I was eighteen. On that day my life changed forever, and I found a love so strong it set me free.

I was born on an island to a woman who was afraid of the outside world. My mother, for reasons she never told me, was terrified of the lands and people beyond our island, so had chosen to raise her daughter far away from them, where she would be 'safe.'

Sometimes, she would mention my father, but moments like that were rare, and always laced with fear. She would never tell me anything about the lands beyond our island, no matter how often I begged.

I was curious, at first. I wanted to explore the world for myself, instead of visualising it in daydreams. But as the years passed, I started to believe what my mother told me—that she had hidden us from the world because there was nothing for us out there but hate, danger, and pain.

My mother died soon after my eighteenth birthday, leaving me only her fear of the unknown. And so, I was alone . . . sort of. Every week, a tradesman by the name of Mo would travel to my Island on a rowboat with a box of food, water, clothes and other useful items. In return for these things, my mother, and now me, would make nets out of twine and mend the old ones Mo would bring to be fixed. My mother and Mo had come to an agreement, that they would never speak to each other, no matter what, and I kept this promise now my mother was gone. So, in a way, I was alone.

Until the girl came.

It started like any other day. It was evening, and I was sitting in my mother's old rocking chair, its old wood creaking as I rocked back and forth, mending old fishing nets and making new ones to sell. My fingers, long and nimble, are perfect for stitching and weaving, and the nets I made were strong. I tested each net myself, normally catching a few fish for supper as I did.

As I sat on the rocking chair by the window, I glimpsed the weather outside. Storm clouds filled the sky, and thunder shook the walls of my old wooden house. The waves, once so calm and peaceful, was now punching and beating the rocks around my island with all their might. This was unusual for this time of year. Storms normally came in winter, not summer, as it was now.

Looking back down at the net, I felt a sudden urge to head out into the storm; to feel the rain against my face, to watch the sea rise and fall around me. The wind was blowing so hard it would knock me off my feet, I knew this, but I didn't care. I loved watching storms. I loved seeing the waves turn wild and unforgiving. It made me feel free. I shivered with excitement at the thought of braving the storm and put the fishing net down. The nets could wait. I had a whole week to make them, and I knew, deep inside, that if I didn't go out, I would miss out on something extraordinary.

I stood and draped an old brown trench coat over my wide shoulders and caught a glimpse of myself in the mirror that hung by the door. My skin is dark ebony, and my hair an unruly tangle, yet as soft as feathers. My arms are strong from years of fishing by the shore with nets I keep for myself, from rebuilding the parts of the house that break with age, and from the life that I have made.

A lonely life, my inner voice whispered, sad and melancholy, yet endurant. *But a life, nonetheless. What other choice do I have?*

I wrapped my coat around myself and, taking a deep breath, walked out into the storm. When I reached the shore, the storm was stronger, with a gale that screamed its fury under dark clouds. The few gulls still flying were tossed like paper in the storm, flashes of white in the grey, tumbling as they struggled against the force of the tempest.

I started to sing. I don't know why I sang then, but it felt like the right thing to do. The sound of my voice relaxed me and made me feel less alone. For a moment, I thought I felt the storm calm. But soon my hair was drenched, and my fingers numb. I turned to go inside, to get warm, ignoring the embarrassment I felt at singing to a storm. Then I hear a sound, a cry of pain, one long note piercing the darkness.

It came from the other side of the island, behind one of the lonely trees. At first, I thought I must have misheard it, but then I heard the voice again; wailing, sobbing, crying out in pain. Slowly, I walked across the island, leant my head around the trees blocking my view, and gasped at what I saw.

Wearing a top made of shells and woven nets, with golden bracelets around her wrists, and eyes the colour of honey, I saw a girl. The most beautiful girl I have ever seen. Her skin was the golden brown of a sunset, and her ringlets twice as long as my own Afro, and as black as night. But none of this was as shocking as her tail. From the waist down, she had a purple and blue fish tail, long and glimmering even in the darkness of the storm around us. A deep gash dripped blood down the side of her tail, and scratches marked her body.

I'd read stories of mermaids and mermen but hadn't believed them. Who would? But here was a mermaid, with eyes the colour of honey, and lips as pink as the broken shells around us.

Slowly, I walked forward, keeping my hands out in front of me to show her I meant no harm. She heard me approach and looked up; eyes wet with tears, curious but fearful. No creature this beautiful deserved pain, so I smiled and knelt down beside her, keeping my voice soft, but loud enough that she would hear me over the gale.

"Hello," I said. "You're hurt, will you let me help you?" She didn't reply. "Can you speak?"

She looked at me confused, her tears shining in the light from the windows of my house.

I motioned to her tail, and the gash dripping blood, and then pointed back to my house, trying to make her understand that I could help her. Her eyes let me know she understood, and with a nod she wrapped her arms around my neck as I lifted her.

I took her back to my house and laid her on the sofa, draped a blanket over her shoulders, and brought out the medical kit I kept in the kitchen. I stitched and wrapped her gash, and once I'd finished, I dressed the rest of her cuts and gave her one of my jumpers to keep her warm.

I sat beside her and pointed at my chest. "Hazel. My name is Hazel."

The girl nodded. Her voice was racked from disuse, and each sound took a lot of effort. "H . . . Hazel?"

"Yes!" I smiled.

The girl smiled too, then pointed at her chest. "M . . . M . . . Maeve."

"Maeve," I repeated, then we smiled together.

Maeve spent the next few weeks living with me as she healed, hidden from Mo's sight inside the house. I cooked for her; Jollof rice, jerk chicken, fried plantains, and my other favourite meals, all of which she relished. I told her about the life I had made, and what little of my past there was to know, about my mother and my life growing up alone. Slowly, as time passed, Maeve learned my language, as it turned out Merpeople have their own. As she learned to understand and be understood, I learned more about her.

She didn't have a family and had been swimming alone out in the ocean when she was caught in the storm, cutting herself on the rocks around my island. If I hadn't gone outside and sang to the storm, she would never have heard my song, and called out for help, and I would never have seen her.

"You . . . have beautiful . . . voice." She told me one day. "Heard you . . . sing . . . beautiful."

As she healed, I started taking her to the sea, and we swam together. It was wonderful to watch her laugh as her tail healed, and to have someone to talk to. In return for my kindness, she taught me how to swim stronger and faster, and she told me stories of the world beyond my island.

The day we had our first kiss, I realised I was in love.

One day, a year after we first met, Maeve asked me, "Why do you stay on this island?"

I took a deep breath and told her the secret, which I had even denied myself. "I could leave. I could build a raft and never look back," I said, holding her close as we sat by the shore, watching the sunset turn the blue sky to gold. "But I was scared that my mother was right, that it's dangerous out there, and there is nothing and nobody for me. But now . . ." I turned and look into her honey-coloured eyes. "Now I know that, if I could leave, I wouldn't. All I need is here with you, Maeve."

"It is dangerous," Maeve said. "But everything has a small amount of danger. The world can be a wonderful place, as long as you know where to go."

We sat in silence for a moment, until Maeve said, "What if there was somebody who could show you the world? Would you go?"

"Yes, but only if it was you," I said, and we kissed.

A week later, Maeve said she had to go, but she wouldn't tell me why.

"I will come back to you, I promise," she said.

I believed her, and, even though it almost broke me to do so, I let her go. I couldn't make her stay. I loved her too much for that.

For weeks I felt nothing; no joy, no sadness, just loss. Nothing was interesting enough to keep my attention. And I spent every waking hour watching the shore for Maeve. As I walked to the shore to spend another day watching for my lost love, I heard her voice as she called my name. I ran to the shore, heart pounding, and there she was, tail flapping in the water, one hand holding a rope attached to a small rowing boat.

"When you're ready," she said.

"I can't. What if I don't belong out there?" I cried.

"Sometimes we must lose ourselves to find ourselves," she whispered, gripping my hand tightly in hers. "And it doesn't matter what other people think. You deserve to belong."

With tears in our eyes, we held each other close.

"Thank you," I said, pressing my forehead against her own. "Will you stay with me?"

"Always, and forever," she replied.

"Then I'm ready."

And so, my story began.

Pipi the Panda

By Emma Bowler
Eight years old from Dartford, England

Deep in the bamboo forest lived a panda called Pipi. She was lonely because she didn't have a friend, so she decided to set out and find one.

Soon enough, she saw a beautiful bird flying overhead. Surprisingly, it swooped down and perched on to the tree next to her! Suddenly, it started to speak.

"Are you okay?"

"I would like to fly like you," Pipi said.

So, the bird offered to help her. They made wings out of leaves and Pipi climbed up a tree to test them. She then jumped off, but instead of flying, she fell and landed with a THUMP!

The bird rushed over but it was too late, Pipi was already gone.

Pipi was walking through the trees feeing lonely and sad. She suddenly heard fast footsteps coming her way then, in a cloud of dust, a cheetah appeared in front of her.

"Do you need any help?" the cheetah asked.

"I would like to run like you," Pipi said.

"Okay, try and run as fast as me," the cheetah said, but Pipi couldn't keep up.

The cheetah hurried back to see if she was okay but Pipi was already gone.

Pipi was walking through the trees when she heard someone coming her way. She saw a green head poking out of the leaves. Suddenly, a tortoise came out and stared up at her.

In a croaky voice he asked, "What are you doing?"

Pipi replied, "I want to be just like you."

The tortoise helped her to find the right size coconut shell and put it on her back. But it fell off! The tortoise clomped over but Pipi was already gone.

Pipi was wandering aimlessly through the trees when she saw a rabbit holding a carrot coming towards her.

The rabbit stopped and asked, "What are you doing?"

Pipi replied, "I want to be just like you."

The rabbit helped her to find sticks. He put them on Pipi's head, so they would look like rabbit ears, but they fell off. The rabbit ran to pick the sticks up and help but Pipi was already gone.

Pipi was walking miserably by the river. She sat down and gazed at her reflection thoughtfully.

Suddenly, there was a rustle in the trees and Pipi saw all of the animals she had met earlier.

The animals asked, "Would you like to be our friend?"

Pipi replied, "But don't I have to be the same as you to be your friend?"

"Of course not!" the animals said. "It's okay that we're all different."

The animals crossed the river towards her and from then on Pipi was never lonely again.

The Talent Show

By Emma Bowler
Eight years old from Dartford, England

Deep in the jungle, where the animals lived, was a monkey called Banana. He had auditioned for the annual jungle talent show but there was just one problem—he didn't have a talent!

He had tried absolutely everything but he just didn't know what to do! In the end, he went to his friend Baby Bear's house to ask for some advice.

"I'm doing what I'm best at," Bear said.

"What's that?" Banana asked.

"Growling!"

So Banana thought he'd give it a try, but poor Banana just couldn't do it, so off he went to try something else.

Next, he went to see Flamingo.

"What are you doing for the talent show?"

"I'm doing what I'm best at," Flamingo said.

"What's that?" Banana asked.

"Dancing!"

So Banana thought that he should try it. At first he was quite good at spinning on his tail . . . well, until he fell flat on his face!

"Maybe you try something else," Flamingo suggested.

So off he went to try something else.

Soon, he arrived at Parrot's tree.

"What are you doing for the talent show?"

"I'm doing what I'm best at," Parrot said.

"What's that?" Banana asked.

"Squawking!"

Banana thought he'd give it a try but it was no use, he just couldn't do it! Now, this made Banana quite cross because there was only one friend left to ask and that was Elephant.

Banana finally got to Elephant's stream. He showed Banana how to blow water out of his trunk. So, Elephant and Banana sucked up water and pointed their noses in the air. Banana really hoped that this would work but when he tried to squirt water nothing came out of Banana's nose.

Time was running out because the talent show was in a few hours and Banana still didn't know what to do. He thought that he should just give up, so off he went, swinging through the trees.

Suddenly, Elephant called out, "Stop! I have an idea."

Banana stopped and listened because Elephant always spoke such wise words.

"You should swing for the talent show since you're so good at it."

"What a great idea!"

So off he went off to practice.

Soon, the big evening came and the talent show was all ready . . . and so was Banana! All his friends were brilliant but then it was Banana's turn and he was so excited. It was all worth it in the end because he was amazing. He was better than the best gymnast, soaring higher than the most amazing acrobat. In fact, he was sad when it ended.

Finally, after all the other acts had performed it was time to announce the grand winner! And would you guess who came first?

Wait for it . . .

BANANA!

He was so happy. All his friends believed that with the effort he put in to find his talent he really deserved it.

Dragon Quest

By Thomas Johnston
Eleven years old from Armagh, Northern Ireland

This was the day I had been dreading and it was finally here. Today I had to do a test and if I succeeded I would become a knight and then I'd have to go on my first quests to kill dragons.

Unlike everyone else I liked dragons but they all wanted to destroy them and wipe them off the face of the earth. I wanted to save them and let them exist. I couldn't fail.

Eventually, just before the test commenced a man raced in yelling, "Help! Dragons! There's a giant fire-breathing Dragon in the swamp."

"Is there indeed?" asked the King, who had been watching from the side-lines. "Well, I'll send my bravest knights to kill it." And with that he strode off.

I knew I had to do something but I didn't know what. Then I had an idea. I raced off to the stables where I grabbed the King's Pegasus and freed it before I hopped upon its saddle. It raced off, taking to the sky, however the archers on the castle walls spotted us and shot at the winged horse's tail. The Pegasus fell from the sky onto the forest floor where it landed with a thud.

I had no choice but to continue on foot. I came by a peculiar little green man with large, pointed ears. He beckoned me closer but when I approached him he attacked me and bit my arm. I fought back and kicked him into a river. Now I was terrified! Who knows what else was lurking in the forest?

I came to a clearing. I thought it was the perfect place to stop and have a rest but something huge flew towards me out of the sky. It was much too big to be a bird and it had horns. It swooped and appeared to be some sort of winged bull. I ran off but it was gaining on me fast. Just in time, I reached the trees and spotted a stone path leading out into the swamp.

I had made it! And sure enough there was the dragon. Its eyes were pools of red hot lava and it was staring straight at me. Suddenly, I heard clopping behind me. I leapt into a bush as three knights on horseback arrived. Their swords were gleaming in the sunlight. I leapt out of my hiding place, grabbed a rock and bashed the first knight over the head with it. He collapsed on to the ground. I ran at the second knight, however he deflected my rock with his shield. Before he could attack, I jumped on the dragon and we flew off into the sunset and to a new life.

How My Dream Came True

By Honor Dent
Ten years old from London, England

My name is Dorothy Wellard and ever since I was four years old I've had a dream to become a fireman. I dressed in fireman clothes at school, at home and even wore them to bed!

My father was very supportive of my dream, always telling me to never give up. However, my mother thought women were supposed to stay in the kitchen and not put out fires. Looking back, I realise that she just wanted to keep me safe.

I told this to the man interviewing me at the fire station and much to his annoyance, he could see I was determined and would not give up. He put me through a vigorous training camp, hoping I would fail, but I didn't.

I beat all the men there. So they had no choice but to hire me.

As much as I loved my job, there were issues. Working in an all-male fire station meant that I was often ignored. Unless, of course, my colleagues wanted a cup of tea—then they would speak to me!

I was brought along if there was a fire but I was told to stay in the lorry, or talk to the crowds that gathered at fires, or deal with the people affected by the fire, but never once was I allowed to do what they considered to be a 'man's job' like putting out the fires. This was frustrating!

Billy, the most popular but worst fireman, always told me in his low gruff voice, "Dorothy, you should be a secretary or a teacher. That's what women do."

Why can't all men be like my father?

One day, when I was at home with my parents, the phone rang and it was my boss.

"Get down here this instant!" he yelled. "There's a fire at the old warehouse on Killick Street!"

I was shocked and stood motionless like a cold marble statue. My boss was actually phoning me—including me?

"Hello? Hello? Dorothy?" he screamed.

"Yes, of course. I will be there in five minutes. Thank you, sir!" I said.

I put the phone down and ran to the car. My mother watched me, shaking her head.

When I reached the warehouse it was chaos. People were shouting and a woman was screaming that her child was trapped inside the warehouse. My boss was pacing back and forth and I ran up to him, eager to help.

"There's a child trapped, so please deal with the mother," he snapped.

My heart sank like a stone carelessly thrown in a lake. He wasn't giving me a chance after all. He turned towards Billy who ran over to us.

"We can't fit through boss!" Billy said.

"I'll go!" I exclaimed.

"NO!" they shouted in unison.

"You can't do it, it's too dangerous!" Billy said.

But an innocent child shouldn't die.

Whilst no one was looking I slipped into the warehouse and found the tiny gap in the collapsed wall. Thick smoke hung heavy in the air. I could hardly breathe. The deadly poisons caused my eyes to water, making me stumble. After a few despairing moments, I came across a small girl, around four years old, lying on the ashy floor. She was unconscious and barely breathing.

During my training, I had learnt the fireman's lift, but until now my skills had not been required. My heart was pounding. The smoke was getting heavier and thicker by the second.

I lifted the young girl up on to my shoulder. Staggering towards the exit, I tried to stay below the smoke. I squeezed through the hole and ran for the door. I heard a big groan and as I exited, the burning building took her last gasping breath and fell to the ground, with a small explosion.

The child and I were momentarily covered by a huge dust cloud and I couldn't breathe. We were immediately surrounded by people.

The mother was crying and wrapped me in a tight hug whispering, "Thank you, thank you, thank you!"

"You disobeyed orders!" growled my boss.

"But—" I wanted to argue but suddenly the world started to tilt and as I fell into the darkness the last thing I saw was my boss' face screwed up in a scowl.

*

When I woke up, I was in hospital. My mother was crying in the chair next to the bed and my father was pacing anxiously back and forth. There was no sign of any of my colleagues or my boss.

I was only in hospital for one night. Before I left, I visited the little girl I had saved. Her name was Jane and thankfully someone was helping her and her mother to find a new home.

The next day I made my way into work with a heavy heart. This was it, I was going to be fired. I had disobeyed orders but I wasn't sorry though. To save Jane's life, it had been worth it.

No-one made eye contact with me as I approached. I made my way, very slowly, up the stairs to my boss' office. My feet were so heavy like they were made of concrete.

My boss rose out of his chair when I knocked. I started talking immediately, "I am not sorry for saving a life and would do it again given the chance."

My boss frowned.

Here it comes, I thought.

I looked up and my boss was smiling.

"I don't want to fire you! That's the last thing I want to do, Dorothy. The bravery you showed at the fire was outstanding and it showed me that I have been wrong to keep you from fighting the fires. I'm sorry. From now on you will be right in the thick of it. If anyone causes you problems you send them to me. You're a hero!"

I couldn't believe my ears. Maybe I was hallucinating because of inhaling all that smoke?

My boss then said that he had put me forward for an award for my bravery. I didn't need or want an award—I was just doing my job—but I accepted as I thought it would show all the young girls out there that they could be firemen too if they wanted.

*

Five years later, when my boss retired, I was promoted to fire chief! I was finally the boss of my local fire station at Tebay. By then there were women in a number of stations around the country (although separate showers for women in fire stations took a lot longer).

So, if you ever face the same dilemma as me, don't stand there and do nothing or just accept it. There is only one option really. Fight! Fight for the chance to prove yourself, for what is right. Be brave, be bold and be fearless!

A Seed's Tale

By Chloe Evans
Eleven years old from Inverness, Scotland

I live in a flower and I don't wish to be boastful, but it's probably the most beautiful flower of them all. Most people consider it as a weed, but to me it's a home. That's right, I live in a dandelion.

It's not just me though, I live with many other brothers and sisters, and sure, my siblings can often be irritating, but I love them just the same. There are lots of us and we're waiting for a very special day. We've been counting the days the sun rises and everyone is incredibly excited for the day when we become part of the glorious wind and are swept away to create new flowers all over the field—everyone except me.

I don't want to leave our little safe haven, our clump of paradise hidden deep in a flower. I'm scared we'll be trodden on when we eventually land on soft grass, or maybe we won't land at all! What if we land on thorns or in a bog? I have heard lots of horror stories of seeds not making it to the right place.

Finally, the dreaded day has come. Everyone else was waiting impatiently for the wind to become strong and yelling, "Hurry up" or "Come on wind."

I was glad the wind wasn't picking up, and secretly began to hope that maybe we didn't have to go.

Suddenly, the wind began to SWOOSH and SWISH and blow harder and harder. There was lightning and huge rumbles as though there was an earthquake in the sky and suddenly there was pounding rain. The wind roared like a savage beast.

I wanted to scream, but I'm a seed, and it's common knowledge that seeds can't talk, and we can't scream either. I was blown this way and that, not certain where I was. I attempted to look below, but I was quickly swept away again in a different direction, then everything went dark.

I woke up and there was a glowing sun to greet me, as always. For a minute everything was normal. Then I remembered I wasn't in my flower and I felt absolutely terrible. I knew being swept away wasn't a great journey that all seeds had to take. It was a death sentence.

I scanned my surroundings and noticed I had landed in a barren field of dirt, and I was right next to a giant? Was it a spud? I couldn't tell.

Where was I? It certainly wasn't a field of luxuriously soft grass, that's for sure. Then I heard a huge thump that seemed to shake the ground beneath me. I stayed perfectly still, trying my hardest not to attract any attention.

THUMP. THUMP.

The noise was getting closer. I saw an enormous pair of pink wellington boots coming towards me. What was going on?

A voice from far above me squeal with delight. "Mummy, Mummy, I found a seed. We talked about them at school! It's so small."

The voice continued to chatter away but that wasn't my main concern at that moment, it was the giant hand lowering down to grab me! It picked me up in an uncomfortable warm hand and started running with me towards a huge red house I'd never seen before. The thing dropped me several times before it reached the house. Ouch!

"Mummy, look, Mummy!" the creature carrying me cried.

Another one of them but taller came out of the big red house and walked over to see.

"Mary? Is everything okay," the bigger one asked.

"Look, it's a seed, and it grows into a pretty flower. We learnt that at school Mummy!"

"How on earth did you find one tiny seed in such a huge potato field?"

"Because it looked like the seed from the pictures at school. Can I keep it? Can I?"

"Of course! I'm sure it will look lovely when it grows."

"Yay!" squealed the creature holding me, jumping up and down with excitement.

That's when my new life began. I began to crave sunlight and water, and a little bit of soil wouldn't hurt either. I also longed for a dark space to crawl into and hide. I was given my very own clay pot on the window, and a very nice spot on the windowsill with lots and lots of sunlight. I was watered and well looked after and I absolutely loved my new life.

I grew taller and felt different, not-so-small, more majestic. Gradually, I was turning into my old home! So this is what happens when the wind picks you up! Maybe my brothers and sisters are in their own clay pots, in other big red houses.

One day, Mary, the little girl who had brought me here, got home from school. Her mummy sat down and sighed.

Mary yelled excitedly, "Mummy it's a pretty flower!"

Mummy stood up and took a closer look.

I suppose they had been so busy, they hadn't noticed how much I'd grown.

Mummy slapped her hand to her mouth and cried, "It's a weed! I had no idea. If I'd had known we wouldn't have grown it. Let me get the weed killer, and we can throw it out."

Mary began to cry, tears dripped down her cheeks.

Mummy gave her a hug. "What's wrong?"

"It's not a weed mummy, it's a flower. Please don't kill it."

"Darling, we can't grow a weed in our house."

"Why not?"

Mummy paused and then said, "I suppose you've got a point."

"Please Mummy."

Mummy looked into her eyes and melted. When she turned to face me, she seemed to see me in a whole new light. "I suppose you're right, it is rather beautiful, isn't it?"

That my friends is my tale, and I'm very happy I've told you it, because there's something you should know. If you see a little seed sitting on the ground, pick it up, and give it a home, because every seed has a tale to tell, and you might just feel better when you go to sleep that night.

For that is my story . . . what's yours?

The Last Plane Home

By Andrew Wyles
Fourteen years old from Aberdeen, Scotland

It was a cold, black winter's night. Snow drifted past the window of my small studio apartment. The clock struck 11 o'clock. It was time. I packed my bag with the essentials: snacks, water and extra clothes. I left the apartment block and trudged down the street towards the airport. A newspaper floated towards me.

1942
ST PETERSBURG UNDER HEAVY SIEGE DUE TO GERMAN FORCES

I swiped it away and continued walking. The smell of burning rubber filled my nostrils. The factories and industrial buildings were just around the corner. In the distance you could hear the quiet whir of machinery as the factory employees worked on through the night.

Before I arrived at the airport, I stopped at a phone box and called my colleague Boris.

"Hello?" he said.

"Hi Boris, it's Alex. Sorry to be calling you so late but I think I'm done with my investigations."

"What were you looking into again?"

"Mysterious disappearances of other politicians and reporters like me. One of my colleagues has now gone missing as well and I'm afraid that I might be next," I said.

"Well, what are you going to do? The city is on lockdown because of the German forces. No one's allowed in or out," Boris said.

"I'm getting the last flight out of the country and it's going to India. It's currently under control by the Allies so I'll be safe. I will keep in touch."

I hung up and walked into the airport. After going through the security checks, I followed the other passengers along the runway. Out of the corner of my eye I saw six rectangular boxes being boarded into the cargo hold.

Why would they be loading boxes on when this is just a passenger plane? Surely it should only be regular suitcases being boarded?

I put the thought to the back of my mind as I boarded. I was exhausted. After getting seated and settled in I went straight to sleep.

I woke up two hours later needing to go to the toilet. Whilst waiting in line I thought I recognised an African reporter called Nimbad Namoot. I was about to greet him, when the bathroom door opened and it was my turn. I stopped when I heard voices coming from the cargo hold below.

"We need to act quickly . . . prepare the coffins . . . lure him down here."

What are they talking about? Are there really coffins on the plane? That must have been the strange boxes I saw being loaded on to the plane. But why?

After I'd finished in the bathroom, I returned to my seat and kept an eye on the cargo hold entrance. Within moments, two men emerged. One was tall and stocky with an eye patch and bruised skin. His hair was as black as the night sky and he was scruffily dressed. When he smiled, you could see that he had several teeth missing, and the ones that he did have were stained yellow. The other was the complete opposite; small, skinny and neatly dressed.

I made my way quickly to the back of the plane and found a hatch leading to the cargo. I prised it open as quietly as I could and dropped down into the cargo hold without anyone noticing. The first thing that hit me was a smell like rotten flesh. I was in a small dark room. Documents and letters were strewn over the floor. A single lamp lit the cramp area. How could anyone work in this environment?

There was a letter on the floor. I picked it up and immediately knew something was wrong. It was addressed to a well-known member of the Gestapo: Alfred Fischer. The letter instructed Alfred to sell plane tickets to all the Russian reporters, politicians and influential people in St Petersburg, but for half the price, and it would take them out of the country. The plan was to kill them when they were on the plane and dump the bodies when they got to their destination.

My blood ran cold when I saw the signature at the bottom of the letter.

Yours Sincerely, Adolf Hitler

Without thinking I ran but in the wrong direction so I was further into the hold. I stopped when I ran past six big crates in the middle of the room. Only, they weren't crates, they were coffins. I opened the first coffin and to my horror I recognised the face of one of the missing politicians.

The next four were the same. Each contained one of the missing people whose disappearance I had been investigating. There was one last coffin. I pushed up the lid and looked in. It was empty apart from a note inside.

Alexander Antonov
6 ft 1
skinny build, reporter

That was me.

A Golden Promise

By Emma Uren
Eighteen years old from Auckland, New Zealand

Rain shattered across the rooftops.

"Ugh, it's started again."

I could feel that slightly prickly, sweaty feeling that always comes when rain starts to creep along my arms.

"You should be thankful for the rain, Adegoke. Only a few months ago you were complaining that it was too dry, Blessing, our head housekeeper said as she crossed the room to draw the blinds.

"Yeah, well, now I wish it would stop."

I rolled over. The crunch of beanbag beans swirled under my stomach. The view beyond the windows was a bleak picture these days: our courtyard filled with mud, the air shining with heat or striped with rain. Even the pool was muddy—not that I needed a swimming pool in this weather. At least we had air conditioning. On the hottest days I barely left our compound.

"You've been playing on that thing all day. Isn't it time for your studies?"

I groaned, and flopped my arms against the beanbag, dropping my Gameboy on to the carpet. "Do I have to?"

Blessing's voice was stern. "You're the son of a king, Adegoke. You have to set a good example."

"I bet Papa didn't study after dinner when he was my age," I muttered.

Blessing raised an eyebrow. "What was that?"

"Nothing!" I gathered up my Gameboy and retreated to my room.

Mama and Papa were home for a change, and I didn't want any disagreements this early in the evening. Right now they were probably in the West Wing, discussing riots and politics and other boring stuff with the advisors.

I lay on my bed and stretched. Last week we had moved here suddenly from our palace in Abuja. We didn't normally move during the wet season, and I wondered if maybe my parents had had a disagreement. I twisted the ring on my finger. Everybody was so tense these days. It was getting on my nerves, and the rain, too. As if it could hear me, the pounding on the screen door grew louder. I groaned and shut my eyes. Stupid rain.

*

I was woken in the night by loud noises. At first I thought it was the rain again, but then I realised that the banging and shouting was coming from inside the compound.

Suddenly, the door opened and Blessing ran in.

"Adegoke! Quick, get up," she hissed. "The compound's being attacked."

I stumbled out of bed and grabbed a jacket from the floor. The tang of smoke tugged at my nostrils.

"What's happened? Where are Mama and Papa?"

I looked up to see in surprise that her eyes were glistening in the darkness. Blessing was crying.

"They've been . . . they were . . . killed by the attackers. Everyone's dying—oh, they'll kill you too if they find you. I'm sorry. I'm so sorry. There's been so much political tension. We were all worried but I can't believe it's come to—here, take this." She wiped her cheeks angrily and shoved some money at me, then scribbled an address on some paper. "Go to my cousin's house in Lagos. He'll help you get out. Oh, and take these clothes so nobody can recognise you, you hear me? Be strong, my Prince."

She hugged me, then pushed me towards the screen doors to my ground-floor balcony. Still sleepy, I staggered forwards and caught the handle. It was strangely cold. Surely this was all a strange and terrible dream. I turned back, wanting to say something.

"Go!" she shouted and I ran.

*

The man at the desk had greasy hair and a cigarette burn in his shirt—the sort of person I would never normally speak to. It was strange how quickly everything had changed. Still, after sleeping rough in the city, I probably didn't look much better.

The sign outside this shop had been scribbled with rust, but still proclaimed the words it had taken me two bus rides and a fifty minute walk to find: Internet Café. Quality connection.

I pulled my jacket tighter and approached the desk. My legs felt like jelly.

"Could I use the internet, please?"

The man looked me up and down. "That's 150 naira an hour."

It cost money?

That was something I hadn't expected. All the same, I dug in my pockets, pulling out the crumpled notes that Blessing had handed me a lifetime ago. A hundred and fifty gone. That meant less than two thousand left.

How long would I last on two thousand?

I handed the money over. The man's gaze seemed to burn through my clothes and skin like acid, as if at any second it would melt away my disguise and he would know who I really was. Papa's words came floating back to me ... *the people are unhappy ... riots in Gboko ...* but this time the words were suffocating, dangerous, alive.

"Fine. You have one hour. You'd better be out by quarter past, kid."

I nodded and scurried away to a computer, feeling a little less jelly-like.

It had taken so much effort to get to an internet café that I had barely thought about what I would do once I got here. First, I tried sending messages to friends. Mostly I didn't know their contacts, but there were a couple I remembered. I researched bus routes to Lagos. I started to look up the news, but figured that was probably a bad plan. I had an idea. It was a bit desperate. But hey, I was a bit desperate. Who knows it might even work?

One of my friends had gone to England on holiday last year, and said that people overseas were very nice. Mama had always told me to ask when I needed something. Why couldn't I ask them for help?

I opened a new email and started typing in random addresses.

And for the message—what to say? How could I convince anyone to help me? Right now I wished more than anything I had paid more attention in my English classes. How would I describe my situation? Desert … no. Despair … no. Desperate. Yes, desperate! That was a good word to use. I remembered that one now.

Imperfect or not, I typed on, pushing through the broken phrases. My tutor and I had been doing letter-writing just two days before … before things fell apart.

I started the email, then frowned. I should offer something in return—nobody would help me otherwise. I was sure Papa had once talked about money somewhere in Switzerland.

Dear Friend,
I am Adegoke a Nigerian Prince. I am in great turmoil in my country as my relatives are dead and there are riots. I desperately need money to leave but if you will help me my family has gold in the bank. I will reward you greatly. Please help!!
Your humble servant,
Adegoke

I sighed and pressed my fingertips to my forehead. It would help. I had to keep telling myself that. I was sure it was the right thing to do. Surely, somebody, somewhere would reply.

Outside, dusk was collecting against the grimy windows. Beyond the glass, I could see the last rays of the setting sun spiderwebbing their way towards the horizon. A golden promise, trickling away.

Far From The Home I Love

By Amy Lever
Nineteen years old from Manchester, England

Four walls stare back at me in semi-darkness. I can just about make out their crevices by the light that has managed to migrate from the window and become displaced in their corners and cracks.

A hand reaches out in a sheepish morning stretch towards this light, only wanting to feel its warmth, but casts a shadow instead. I hear a neck, an arm, a weary leg crack, crack as they rise and move after being still for so long.

Crack, crack like the glow sticks my grandmother used to bring me on bonfire night when I was too young to hold a sparkler. I am standing and my perspective has changed from the walls to my window.

"To the window to the wall," the soundtrack of my life chants.

How exciting. I have not physically moved in days. Instead I travel in cracks, slips, nooks, crannies and corners. This is my new favourite pastime; they never move, they are still like me, yet they change when light is shed on them.

Stillness, grief does that apparently or at least that's what I heard my mother say through the crack in my door when she must have thought I was asleep. If this is grief then it is very boring.

I watched an episode of *The Simpsons* once, prior to my wall crack watching days, where Homer sped through five whole stages of grief in the span of thirty seconds. I should have known that my experience would not be the same as a cartoon yellow man; mine is monotonous and singular. There are no stages, no episodes, only one long, dull drawl.

The hand pulls back the curtain and reveals my window and windowsill with the cactus plant that sits on it, set against the backdrop of a drizzly grey morning. No wonder light wants to occupy my cracks when it is clearly unwelcome in such gloom. I have the sudden urge to press myself against the window to feel coolness spread through my cheek, to feel connected to my body for once.

My vision is obscured by a blurred blob in the corner squished up against the glass. This kind of reminds me of when my mum used to try and use our camcorder when we went on holiday. She would capture my own and my sister's sunburnt smiles, which were stretched further by my grandmother's darker and more wrinkled grin. These were obscured by my mother's finger on the lens, which appeared as a blob that was a shade in between us, ironically, as my mother is the generation in the middle as well.

Now I'm on the floor, my view sweeping past me, dropping from ceiling to window to windowsill and finally to the carpet in one swoop. I drop at the thought that I will never really see her again—only sometimes in the face of my mother but never in my own.

The hand moves towards the cactus on the windowsill, the fingers prick themselves on the points of a spine. I will myself to feel distracted by the pain, to own the hand that pulls back the curtain, the legs and neck that crack, the cheek that is smudged up against the window. Or better yet, I will this to be my spindle prick and fall asleep for years and years, uninterrupted by cracks of light and concerned whispers through slips in the door.

I achieve neither; the cactus a haunting reminder of the one who gifted it to me and her parting words as I left with her present to university.

"Don't go feeding it pot noodle," she said. "Just a little water but it will probably be fine as I know you might forget."

I did forget. Yet it endured all of term time and the journeys there and back. It survived as she had said, even its spines continued to grow and all.

Back then I felt like myself but when I came home my grandmother was not there. Now I do not feel like myself. It's like I am in a police station looking at myself through one-way glass; I know her, I see her, I am her, yet I feel nothing she feels. My disposition is as rigid as the glass that separates us and as cold as the glass she pushes her cheek up against.

My excruciating one-way windowpane is my very own bell jar. This must have been how my grandma felt—unseen and unwelcome in a place that had been her home since 1948, sadly now full of barriers to empathy. Her family portraits, primary school records, birth certificate are stacked up high.

My grandmother met my grandpa here. This was his home since December 1938 where he had got a train leaving his parents behind, trading a gold star badge for a gold lion stamped passport instead.

My grandma spoke your language, did your work and gave birth to your children. She burnt wooden men on a bonfire and sang, "God save the Queen" but she was not the colour of the British flag, so you sent her away.

The hands close around the cactus, the spines piercing into my skin. I like to think they might be linked, an odd thought I know, but as the cactus continues to grow away from its native home maybe my grandma continues to survive, somewhere in Jamaica, this place where she was born but not the place she calls home.

The hand places the cactus back on the windowsill, its spines tinged red matching the tips of the fingers; they resemble each other for once. It makes me think that we are all one and the same, me and my grandma and everyone else in the world; even though we look different we all bleed red.

Featured Stories

In All My Dreams

By Maddie Parkhouse
Seventeen years old from Warrington, England

Sometimes, when the sunlight peers through the window in just the right place, it reflects from the mirror and my entire room is bathed in rainbows. The first time I saw it happen, the only possible explanation I had was that it was magic. Even now, when I know a rainbow is nothing more than a trick of the light, I bring my hand up to the light and watch the rainbows dance across my skin.

When I sleep, I dream that my skin is made up of rainbows, a thousand of them stitched together. In my dreams, I'm not in my bedroom. I phase through the walls of my house and float down the stairs to the kitchen, and I'm always greeted by the same sight.

In all my dreams, you are there. You always have your back to me, but I can see the streak of flour on your cheek from the cookies that you are always making. You laugh at something that I can't see, and you tip your head up and pour a handful of chocolate chips into your mouth. No matter what I say or do, you never hear me in my dreams, but I think it's the only place where I ever see you truly happy, so I'm content to just sit on the counter and watch you cook, my legs swinging, shimmering with rainbows and stardust.

Sometimes, the rainbows from my mirror are replaced by a storm outside. On those days, I always feel a little twinge of regret, since I won't see you in the kitchen in my dreams. But that doesn't mean that I don't enjoy the noise the rain makes against the glass—a constant pitter patter, like the footsteps of a loved one walking home, or the heartbeat of the sky. Sure, there's no sun, but the sky is lit up by lightning and the window rattles with the sound of thunder, and I know that it's impossible to have a rainbow without rain.

On a stormy night, I dream that we put on a pair of brightly-coloured wellies and grab a yellow umbrella and run down the street in the torrential rain, jumping in puddles and laughing and dancing. In my dreams there is no one to judge us. There is just you and me, rain dripping down our faces, into our boots, and the feeling of freedom that I have yet to find while awake.

One day, maybe I'll tell you about my dreams. Maybe I'll describe the flour in your hair or the smudge of chocolate by your lips. The way the rain drips down your neck and yet you never shiver. I'm afraid, though, that once I've spoken of the dreams, that they might leave forever. I'm not sure if I could sleep without these million snapshots of you in my mind, of your smiles and your laughter.

Maybe I'll never tell you about my dreams. Maybe I'll try to bring the dreams into wakefulness, instead, so I can etch your smile into my mind and know that I was the person to put it there.

Besides, the weatherman said that there's a storm due tomorrow, and I have an umbrella I'm willing to share.

How The Stars Weep

By Megan Kruger
Fifteen years old from London, England

The moon was bright and it made the sea-slick deck glisten like a mirror reflecting the cosmos. His mother had been right when she told him that a Trojan sky on a clear night was a spectacle to behold. He felt that if he squinted his eyes, he would be able to see the vivid colours of the galaxy beyond this world. But there was no time at all for that.

Edan was not here to sightsee; he was here to fight. On behalf of Menelaus and for the honour of all Greek men, he was determined to serve dutifully and bring victory to all of Greece. Yet the army was just a few hundred yards away from the shores of Troy, and he could practically feel the blood pumping at a brutal pace through his veins. He had never fought before.

Abruptly the aged ship, staggering in its size, halted as it met the bay, and shouts were thrown up into the air. As though in a daze, Edan lowered himself from the boat amongst hundreds of other young men, easing his way down a rickety gangplank and on to the solid ground. Surrounding him immediately was a cloud of noise, muffling his ears and leaving him reeling. He allowed himself to be ushered towards the makeshift encampments being erected further up the beach and nodded to his commander. He was stunned as he was given his orders. Suddenly, he wished he was back on his small, insignificant Greek island, wrapped in his mother's arms in their corn field looking up at their mediocre sky.

As Edan retired that evening, he dreaded the following day but he awoke to the sound of war cries. The Trojans were pouring out from their city gates, hundreds upon hundreds of them, adorned in gleaming armour. A burst of fear welled up in his throat and he had to suppress it, lest he should suffocate.

Edan forced himself to leave the entryway of his tent and prepare for battle. He strapped on his chest plate and armed himself with a bow and arrow—he could not bring himself to fight face to face. He may be accused of cowardice, but he was afraid that his heart would not be able to stand the sight of another falling by his sword. At least from afar, he hoped he would not feel the pain he was anticipating so powerfully.

Edan followed the other archers to their pre-determined vantage point on a nearby hilltop, close to the battleground. Far below, the Greek army charged and Edan swore he felt the sound reverberate in his skull. All these things about war he was sure he would never forget.

The archers began shooting, picking out targets in the crowd of Trojans. A few fell, but not nearly enough. Edan could see that the Greeks were vastly outnumbered. They were doomed before they began. As he hurried to nock his arrow and begin shooting, he felt an arrow whip past his ear and strike a tree in the forest behind him. The archers were also under attack. Before he could do so much as open his mouth to warn the commander, an arrow buried itself in his right thigh. His legs gave in and he crashed to the ground. His chest heaving from shock. Within moments, he lost consciousness altogether.

*

Hours later Edan came to and the first thing he noticed was a desolate mood in the air. Vacant faces were scattered across the campsite. It was apparent that they had suffered a painful defeat in the initial battle. That night was to be one of burial, mourning and anguish.

The sun was setting slowly, tucking itself away behind the walls of Troy, and leaving the miserable army to see by the gloomy light of a dismal, darkening sky.

Edan looked down at himself, inspecting his wound. Cloth had been wound around his thigh to stop an infection, and he could feel salve sealing itself over his skin as it dried—someone must have tended to him during the hours he was passed out. He felt lightheaded and utterly exhausted. The sensation made worse by the dull atmosphere and the cold wind sweeping across the bay, seeping into his bones like ice water. He was pulled into sleep's stifling embrace with agonising slowness.

Edan spent the next week or so resting and allowing his injury to heal. Meanwhile, the Greek army was still fighting on fiercely but with every day that passed, even more funeral pyres were lit. At least three ships full of soldiers had sailed to Troy since that first battle. The Trojans were stronger than King Agamemnon had expected, it seemed.

Guiltily, Edan thought of his comrades, while he lay on his infirmary bed recovering. There were others who fought on and laid down their lives for Greece. So, when he was asked to fight again under the orders of King Odysseus, halfway through the second week, he ignored the ghastly pain piercing his leg and the fright taking over his lungs and agreed to go back into battle.

Apparently, a plan had been hatched. All Edan knew was that he found himself standing on the shore, with fifty other soldiers, while they watched the huge naval ships sail back to Mycenae. The army was then ushered towards a great wooden structure standing at the Trojan gates.

In the dim light of dusk, Edan couldn't discern what it was exactly, just that it had four pillars protruding from the underside of the main body, and wheels. To his surprise, the men in front of him began climbing a ladder and entering the belly of the craft. With tens of soldiers pushing impatiently forward from behind, he had no choice but to follow them.

Inside the structure, it was dark but for slithers of moonlight sliding in from slats in the wood. There was the smell of fresh sawdust and varnish potent in the air, stuffing his nose and making his eyes prick with tears. The men around him looked strong, with intense eyes and battle scars ragged across their arms.

With a jolt of uncertainty, Edan wondered why he was here. Not only was he injured, but he was an archer, and a timid one at that. Edan had no idea what they were inside that wooden prison for, but he was convinced he wasn't supposed to be there. There must have been a mistake.

He tried desperately to get the attention of the General, calling through the cavern and past the toughened warriors, but all he got in return were glares, and a glimpse at the back of the General's helmeted head. A grunt sounded from beside him, and he turned to see a soldier looking at him.

"Just relax, we'll be there soon," the soldier said.

With that, the stranger faced the shell of the room again and fell quiet. Edan was bemused: he had no understanding of what the soldier meant.

Edan was jolted from his perturbed thoughts with movement. He could only speculate how long they had been in the structure for; the light slanting into the space was brighter, but that told him little of the time of day. A creaking of wheels was emanating from below, and the frame was trundling unsteadily forwards. Edan could hear feet moving, and shouts calling out. Inside the belly, all was hushed—the men who Edan remembered had been raucous back at the camp now had stony features, and the Commander had a calloused finger pressed to his lips. It was the Trojans.

Anxiety choked him and Edan started shaking. He was spiralling downwards and fast. He was not ready to fight; he hadn't practised properly.

He wasn't ready.

Before he could begin crying out, he felt a hand on his shoulder. It was the same soldier from the night before. The man said nothing, but the act gave him a small comfort. Edan lowered his head into his own trembling hands and tried to breath slowly and deeply. He wanted to see the stars again. Their constancy and presence made him feel safe.

Eventually, the wooden structure came to a precipitous stop, and the soldiers surrounding him began moving, heaving as one unit towards the trap door leading to the ladder below. His anonymous companion stood to follow the others. Edan was the very last soldier left in the structure, cavernous now with the army out of it. His mouth was dry and leathery. He felt sick.

"What are you doing soldier? Get up and fight!" the commander bellowed at him.

Antipathetically, Edan marched to the trap door and fell into line behind his comrades.

A cold arm of air stole the breath from his lungs as his feet hit the dirt beneath the craft. He caught a glimpse of it: an enormous horse, carved intricately and with astounding accuracy. The Greek army was inside the walls of Troy, at last. The soldiers around him darted outwards from the wooden horse, wielding their swords, and fighting the unsuspecting Trojan soldiers, who seemed to have hauled the horse into the city.

Jarring clangs of metal on metal rang in his ears and Edan's vision blurred. He remembered his older brother's tales of battle, and how glorious it had all seemed when he was a young boy. Now, he felt only terror consume his heart, blood turning cold. He wasn't ready for this.

His eyes focused on a figure moving towards him. The man's face was taut and strained; tears stained his cheeks. For a fleeting moment, Edan wondered if this enemy soldier was the same as him; afraid of wounding others, afraid of becoming a murderer—afraid of death? The thought fled his mind as soon as it entered. He felt sharp steel pierce his heart. The man's face was inches from his own. Their eyes locked, and Edan could see pain reflected back at him. Edan fell to the ground, clutching at his chest. He didn't even get the chance to raise his sword.

And, as he lay there in the dust, his life falling away from him, Edan held on to one last, fading memory, of a play he attended with his family when he was a young boy; as the main character suffered from a fatal wound, the narrator read the words, "And as you lay with blood weeping out of your chest, the cosmos weeps for you."

Lying there beneath the clear, blue Trojan sky, he hoped that some star of this fated cosmos mourned for him too.

Time is Ticking

By Johana Pusuluri
Fourteen years old from Devon, England

"Good luck!"

A swarm of kids gathered and gazed up; eyes swirling with anticipation as Ajay, who was perched on the rickety fence, smiled at them hesitantly. Fear seized his throat and butterflies tumbled in his stomach. He couldn't speak. Instead, he simply nodded at the group, giving them a shaky thumbs up.

Closing his eyes, he remembered what his mother told him every day; that his name meant 'the one who is invincible.'

I'll show them what I'm made of, Ajay thought to himself, as he shut his eyes and pushed himself from the battered fence.

The fence gave an ominous groan but Ajay was safe on the other side, at least for the moment. The fence reminded Ajay of the border between his country India and Pakistan, and the ongoing war between them. As time passed, the situation worsened and more and more soldiers and civilians were killed with every minute. Time really was the greatest thief of all. Ajay's father had been killed whilst fighting for his country and Ajay struggled to find a reason to smile and laugh and embrace the feeling of happiness—except when playing cricket.

Cricket was his father's favourite sport and playing it made Ajay feel closer to him. Cricket was a reminder that his father hadn't left him. Every time he picked up a cricket ball and felt its smooth toughness he had a flashback of his father teaching him how to hold it. Every time he gripped the bat he remembered his father's hand on his, those tender loving hands shifting his around the handle. Everything he knew about cricket came from his father. That's why it was so important to him to retrieve the cricket ball, even if it meant going into the feared field, because he had to make his father proud and, of course, they had to continue their game.

Sand blew around Ajay and the sun shone on the arid, deserted field. Cockroaches scuttled around the rubble and lizards lay lazily in the trees, blinking in the sunlight. His tongue was dry and sweat dripped down his face.

Ajay could hear clinking chains and distinct low growls. The wind whistled to him, as if to taunt him, daring him to move forward. The shadows of the trees swaying in the slight, refreshing breeze danced in front of him, without a care in the world.

Ajay's heart pumped rapidly, a shiver ran down his spine and sparks of fear frequently flickered in his eyes. From the shadows of a manky, ramshackle shed, a huge, slobbery dog plodded towards him with a look of suspicion. With sandy-coloured fur and chocolate brown eyes, the dog's heavy and dusty paws thudded with every step. He came to a halt and spat the cricket ball out, glaring at it. It rolled towards Ajay but it came to a halt midway. The dog continued to glower at the ball.

Didn't it have anything better to do?

Ajay debated whether or not to get the ball or to go back without it but then he heard his father's voice, "Come on, son," and he knew he had to make his father proud. And the fact that the dog just let the ball roll towards him confirmed it. He was going to retrieve it—whatever the cost.

He took a fearful step forward and regretted it almost immediately. The dog gave a low warning growl and his eyes conveyed the same message as they lit up suddenly. His distrustful glare soon returned to the ball.

Ajay ran faster than he had ever done before and skidded to grab the ball. Just as he pushed himself up, the dog wrenched Ajay's shoe right off his foot, yet Ajay just kept running, ignoring the pain of the sharp stones as they pierced his foot. He kept running although he could feel the dog's wet, revolting slobber on his legs.

Suddenly, the rusty chains that had bound the dog for so long broke with a loud snap but still Ajay didn't look back. The dog never stopped snapping at his heels. Ajay hadn't realised how vast the field was until he ran. He felt like a small cat at the tips of a beast's clutches in a completely deserted field the size of the ocean. But as large as it was, Ajay could see the fence nearing.

"Almost there," he comforted himself.

He jumped up on to the fence, nearly missed and was hanging by his fingertips whilst the dog barked and snapped at him.

The dog tried to jump and each time Ajay could feel its breath but it never got him. Ajay pulled himself up, out of the dog's reach and pushed himself back over the fence. Panting, he looked around at his friends who cheered and patted him on the back, congratulating him. They even threw him up and carried him around. He had made them proud.

Had he made his dad proud? Surely he must have. He displayed all the qualities his father valued the most: courage, determination and perseverance. He hadn't given up. But thinking of his father looking down on him hadn't given him any strength. Through the pain of splinters and stones, Ajay was just glad that he was safe.

Something was bothering him. He couldn't stop wondering why the dog let the ball roll in the first place if he didn't want Ajay to have it. The dog practically gifted the ball to him—Ajay hadn't needed to prise the ball from the dog's mouth. The dog just let it roll towards him. Yet, when Ajay tried to get it, the dog had barked relentlessly . . . why?

Tick. Tock. Tick. Tock.

Realisation struck Ajay as sharply as the hands of a grandfather clock when they strike twelve. The ball was a bomb, ready to explode.

The Journey Home

By Nicole Kravstov
Twelve years old from Carshalton, England

I would have to go back. I was lucky enough to have escape but now I could start over and build a new identity for myself. Others didn't get that opportunity. Fighting in the war was a privilege—at least that's what they told me and my brother when we signed up.

"Serve your country; prove that you are both men," our family had told us.

But I was sick of it, sick of everything. I didn't want to be on the front line, sacrificing myself when I knew that we would all end up dying anyway. The war wouldn't end. Armies wouldn't just accept defeat. How did no one understand? We were all being set up to fail and yet I had escaped.

But I had to go back. I had been so caught up with planning an escape route that when the time came, I couldn't find my brother. I got to his quarter, but he wasn't there. I assumed it was his shift, and I left without him. How foolish I had been. Now I needed to go back for him. I couldn't just leave him there—hopeless—just another one of our country's victims promised a good life if we won the war.

I turned around and made a sprint for the gates I had run through not five minutes ago. I was still in uniform (I had neither a chance to change nor anything to change into) and I walked past all the dead bodies, with the gun I stole in my hand, in case anyone crept up on me. I made my way towards our trenches and froze when I found him.

He was lying unconscious; blood oozing out of a gash on his shoulder. I had no time to scream for a medic, and even if I did it would ruin my—our—escape plan. I ran towards a medic tent and grabbed a bandage. Before anyone could question me, I was out of there, carrying my brother while simultaneously trying to wrap up his shoulder. He was lighter than I remembered—it must have been the adrenaline combined with the small rations.

The journey back took almost twice as long as it had when I was by myself, but my brother kept asking if we could rest and with his poor, almost fatal condition, I couldn't deny his wish.

We made it. Together. He was almost back to normal at this point, lively and talkative, and the blood was pouring out less. It was his idea to seek refuge in one of the countryside houses. We could do jobs for the house owners, like milking the cows and collecting eggs, until we had earned enough for a train journey back home, to our beloved mother and sister.

So we worked hard, waking up at six each day to help out for minimum amounts of money. Still, it was all we could do, since we had been stripped of every other option. The only thing keeping us from giving up was the thought of being home, at last. Free from the war and reunited as one happy family.

After a long day of work, we would lie down on our mattresses and my brother and I would talk. It'd be almost like when we were younger, before the war started and our lives were thrown upside down.

"John," he'd ask me. "How much longer? I don't know if I can survive much longer out here."

I used to laugh it off and reply, "Not long, George, another week or so and we'll be back home."

But weeks turned into months, until we lost track of time. It could have been anywhere up to a year before we had saved up enough money for two train tickets. Or perhaps it was merely a few weeks; we didn't know. It was hard to get a train ticket; not many people were willing to sell something to two boys who looked like they should be fighting in the war, and risk getting in trouble with the government. We hadn't thought this part through; we assumed that for the right amount of money people would be willing to do just about anything, but it was clear that the war had changed the country; whether for better or worse was arguable.

If you asked me, it was for the worse. The idea of parents shipping off their sons to fight, with a risk of them not even returning, just so they could 'serve the country' was ridiculous and I didn't see so few could understand that. War and conflict would last forever. No one would be free; we would all be ruled by tyrants, regardless of which country won. But George and I, we didn't give up. We kept searching for anyone who would be able to supply us with two one-way tickets.

I feared for George. Every day he complained about how faint he felt and he looked remarkably pale, more so than usual. But eventually we found a supplier, and we were on our way. The train journey felt amazing; with the windows down, George and I felt the cold air on our skins—freedom. In the moment, we thought that the mishaps were over, but merely seconds later we were proved wrong.

The train conductor, a middle aged man with a white beard and glasses, was pacing up and down the train, checking tickets and ensuring that only people who were allowed to be on the train were on it.

I glanced at George and saw that he was holding out his ticket, so I did the same thing, praying he wouldn't question me about why I was on a train, headed the opposite way to the battlefield, when judging by my looks and physique, I was clearly meant to be 'serving my country.'

Nonetheless, he asked me, "Why are you on this train?" I noticed that his gruff voice didn't match his face.

Thankfully, George said, "We're cleared to visit our family, sir; our mother came down with a possibly deadly virus."

I had never been so appreciative for his ability to lie quickly.

But the train conductor didn't even bat an eyelash and kept looking straight at me. "I asked you a question. Why are you on this train?"

I looked at George questioningly and he shrugged, so I decided to repeat what he said. The train conductor nodded his apologies and continued to walk down the carriage.

"What do you reckon that was about?" I whispered to George. "Him ignoring you, I mean."

Again, George shrugged, and I could feel tiredness overcome my senses. I glanced at George, and his expression mirrored mine. Within minutes, we were both asleep.

I was woken up by the train guard calling out our town name. I shook my brother awake and within minutes we were off the carriage and out of the station. We were nearly free.

"Go without me. I don't know how long I can last," George said. He was stumbling from his drowsiness.

"Nonsense, we're almost there." I frowned; confused as to why George would even think of giving up when we were so close.

I picked him up; earning me confused stares from passers-by. I assumed this was because we were too old to be evacuees, yet too young to have retired. I shook off the stares and made my way home, rejoicing in the idea of seeing my mother and sister in less than ten minutes, and being able to be a happy family again, free from the war's chains.

I looked at George. He seemed to either be asleep, his head resting on my shoulder, or unconscious, which I hoped wasn't the case. I felt a steady pulse, so I assumed he was sleeping. I smiled and continued on my way.

A few minutes later, George awoke.

"We're here," I reassured him gently.

I put him down and he sat up, resting against the side of the house before I knocked on our door three times.

When my mother opened the door, she looked like she'd been crying.

"What are you doing here?" she sniffed.

"Me and George are home." I smiled. "We can all be reunited at last."

At hearing George's name, she broke down, taking deep breaths to try and stifle her sobs. I didn't understand what had happened; was it seeing George standing there, looking pale and sick? Or perhaps she was simply relieved that we were safe?

At seeing my questioning look, she returned it with one of her own and frowned.

"What are you talking about John? George died in the war."

I shook my head. "No, that's not right. He's been with me the whole time."

"It was a few months ago. He was found dead in one of the trenches. I'm sorry, I thought you'd already heard; I thought that was the reason you came home. I—I didn't realise you didn't know."

That was impossible; George was right behind me. I turned around to call him but no one was there. He had simply vanished and in a second my whole world collapsed.

Garam Masala and a Pinch of Home

By Sejal Gautam
Seventeen years old from Reading, England

Rajesh had been in England for six months when Diwali came around. He had been working horribly long shifts at the construction site, rebuilding what the war had brought down. He would reach home with sore feet, blistered hands and little money in his pocket, longing for a cup of Proper Indian Chai and a pistachio biscuit.

October brought a chill to the evenings. Rajesh was bundled up in the only coat he owned, a thick heavy thing he had bought for too much money in one of the shops off the high street. It had been the only one in the area without a 'No-coloured' sign pasted to the window.

He was carrying a paper bag full of groceries—chicken for tonight and leftover vegetables, only half soft and still edible. Sunesh Uncle from the shop had been selling them for almost nothing, and Rajesh was glad to take them off his hands if it meant that Uncle had less produce to throw away tomorrow. Rajesh's family always used all the food they had, down to every carrot stalk and watermelon peel.

When he arrived home, he ignored the endearingly excited looks of his flatmates sat by the door in favour of washing off the grime from work with as little water as possible. He made his way to the kitchen, heaved the two huge pans onto the stove and heated them.

This was his favourite part of the day. He watched with satisfaction as the onions sizzled loudly in the hot oil. Rajesh's knife flew over the soft tomatoes quickly and in they went, spitting oil everywhere, roughly chopped but still doing their job. A wrinkled knob of ginger, a couple of garlic cloves with mould chopped off from the ends. Cubes of chicken in one pan, peeled potato chunks in the other.

Rajesh reached into the unstable cupboard above the tiny stove and pulled out the steel circular box. He wiped off a smudge, most likely caused by someone else, before releasing the latches and pulling off the lid with a flourish.

Seven steel containers and the strong and unmistakeable smell of red chillies, the vivid yellow of turmeric, the deep red of the Kashmiri chilli powder, the sharp cumin seeds and the distinctive brown garam masala. The unique, red star anise and the fragrant green fennel seeds. Finally, in the centre, the stark white salt, a delicately small steel spoon sitting in it.

He counted seven spoons of salt, four spoons of turmeric and three and a half spoons of garam masala before he placed the box gently on the side, ready to use it again.

Back at home, Ma had not coddled him, unlike many of his housemates. She had ensured that her 'Raju' could cook as well as she could. He knew his way around the regional cuisines: tandoori chicken and samosas from Punjab in the North, dosa and idli from the South, and fish curry from the West coast. Frying, coating, rolling, kneading; he could do it all, darting around the stove in the minimal space to touch and taste, adding spoonfuls of chilli powder to one large pan, a handful of yellowed coriander to the other.

When the stove was switched off, flour wiped off the counter and the messy kitchen returned to normalcy, the huge scalding pans were carried carefully into the middle of the room. Two teetering towers of chapatis were placed beside them on the floor, the rich fragrances and warmth in the kitchen a siren call for everyone else to arrive.

All twenty-six men crammed into the damp, hardly big enough kitchen. They all wore their best clothes. Each had carried one flamboyant kurta shirt reserved only for this occasion. The dusty lightbulb flickered above, as they sat against the faded walls of the kitchen, aware of the feast that waited for them, as they lit the ten tealights between them. Tiny shadows from candles danced across the ceiling in the dim room. This was the closest they could come to the colourful clay lamps they would have lit today in India.

Prayers were done, sung in cheerful voices, and smiles were shared. Their esteemed young chef began to make his rounds and the other men waited with an increasing sense of anticipation.

Two chapatis were placed on each mismatched plate. Two, rather than their usual one! Some were lucky enough to have a shining steel plate from home rather than chipped, beaten down china. Next came two ladles of each person's choice of curry, or one of each if you had the luxury of being a non-vegetarian.

Steam curled upwards from each plate, the heady aroma of cardamom with hints of cinnamon bringing with it a sense of nostalgia for every man and boy in the room. Yet, every plate of food remained untouched, however enticing, deep vermillion coloured curry beginning to spread slowly towards folded soft chapatis. They all waited until the last two chapatis were taken and Rajesh sat down at the end of the line with his own food.

Everyone raised their glasses of water in his direction, cheers and whistles filling the room. They watched as Rajesh took the first bite, before following themselves, the divine, earthy flavours of the chilli and cumin perfect with the chapatis.

Loud conversation and merriment wrapped around them, braying laughs, conversations in different dialects, slaps on backs as half a chapati was shared. Together, in such a small place—with these people they had grown to know and love in these last few months—this felt just like being back at home.

Small and Beautiful

By Katie Bates
Ten years old from Pennsylvania, USA

One dusty morning, a young girl called Cynthia saw something creeping through the grass. She silently crawled on her hands and knees towards the small thing. As she got closer, she saw that it was a tiny human with a pretty face and long, slender arms and legs. She had a pair of glimmering purple wings, a long dress made from a wrapped purple tulip petal, and an even smaller lavender crown perched atop her head.

Cynthia followed the small creature to the wooden fence, but when it reached the wood, it seemed to suddenly disappear into the post. Cynthia stood there for a moment, before she shook her head and went back inside. It must have been a trick of the light. How else would she have seen the small creature?

*

Violet Lavender sighed with relief as she slipped into the færies' secret home inside the fence. She had almost gotten caught! There is one major rule of being a færie: You must not get caught! If you do, you become a pet of the Larges, aka the humans. You grow bigger and bigger until you become a Large. You shed your wings and are forbidden from ever entering Cydale, the færie land, ever again.

Violet flew hastily through the underground tunnels until she spotted The Opening, which is a way into Cydale. She slowed to a light flutter, and passed through the gates into the place she called home.

Aedelis, her hometown village in Cydale, was bustling. The skyscrapers with their curved tops were a collage of bright colours. Small, country-like houses lined the busy streets, while the taller ones resided on the side roads. Færies of all different shapes, sizes, and colours walked, ran, or flew above the streets and on the sidewalks. The streets themselves were even busier, with little abstract cars racing each other along them while cyclists and flyers swerved their way through the mix.

Violet lifted off, high above the others, zooming over the roads and taking in the sights off her home village once again. She came to rest in front of a small, modest home. It had a brown, pointed, wicker roof and its body was circular.

Violet opened the wooden door set into the pale pinkish-purple adobe. She set down her basket and called, "I'm home!"

Her voice echoed throughout the house, and she listened for a reply.

She heard the sweet voice of her mother, Lilac Rose, yell back, "I'm here!"

She gave a sharp, almost tweeting whistle, and the family's young dog, Fox came around the corner.

"Hello Fox!" Violet hugged the dog tight and he rolled over on to his back, clearly expecting a belly rub.

Once he had trotted away, Violet ran upstairs to her attic room. It had a low ceiling, but the vast amount of space made up for it. Her bed and dresser in the corners. Her knapsack for school was already packed up and hanging off her desk chair. She grabbed it and opened the window.

She stomped her foot three times to let her mother know that she was leaving. She waited until she heard the three bangs of the metal pot lids that signalled her mother's reply, and then she took flight, closing the window as she went.

She zoomed through the air, high above the other færies, until she came to rest on top of another house. Her best friend, Redwood Chia, was waiting for her. Once again Violet took flight, this time with her friend right beside her.

*

I had to be dreaming, Cynthia told herself as she arrived at school but then she noticed a breeze, a slight disturbance, in the air. She looked up and saw the same glittery purple wings as before! But this time there was also a set of red wings. She stopped walking with her friends and stared at the colours, transfixed by their beauty, until her friends called to her. Then she forced herself to turn.

Cynthia kept her eyes straight ahead as she walked down the hall, once again forcing herself to believe that she had just been dreaming, or that it was just a trick of the pale September light.

Over the next month, Cynthia saw the colours more and more and not just purple and red. From red to teal, aqua to lilac she saw them all.

One day, she went to the library and searched up the tiny creatures. She learned that they were mythical creatures called færies, or fairies. They were supposed to be fictional creatures, but Cynthia knew that that was not true. She learned all she could about these creatures, and then she waited. She had a plan. She was going to catch a færie.

Cynthia finally got her chance. Redwood and Violet were outside in the frosty grasslands, hunting for the perfect piece of tree bark to keep them warm, while they gathered grass for their mothers to weave into winter blankets. Cynthia noticed the red and purple almost immediately against the white, frosty snow.

She pulled out a metal can lined with wool from her pocket and opened the punctured lid and crept forwards. Soon, she was practically on top of the færies. Cynthia leaned down and softly picked up the red-winged færie. She felt its strong magic burn her fingers and yelped dropping the creature in surprise.

Cynthia watched as they flew off, but the red one was moving a bit slower than the purple one. So she grabbed her can again and placed it over top of the færie, caging her in. Once she felt the creature fly up, she slid the lid under the can and turned it over. She held it in her hands and watched and felt a small thump as the færie hit the bottom. Suddenly, Cynthia felt that the can was heavier.

She finally realised that if she kept the færie, it would just keep getting bigger and bigger! Then she would not be small and beautiful anymore.

That's what færies are, she realised. *Small and beautiful.*

Cynthia slid the lid off the can and watched the færie fly away. It began to shrink in size. The faerie joined her purple friend and Cynthia watched them disappear into the fence wood.

Sir Arthur Conan Doyle and the Fairies

By Loveday Lock
Eleven years old from Bridgend, Wales

Frances and Elsie came to take pictures of us again! I was in the middle of breakfast—a delicious buttercup and bluebell sandwich with a mug of morning dew tea. Alas, I had to leave them and run away to hide in an empty acorn shell.

It could have been worse, my friend Masie Moonstone was in the middle of morning exercises on the spider web trampolines. She had to leap out of sight and hang from a foxglove stem until they left after two hours. Her arms even turned from stunning silver to an alarming pink!

"We must get a photograph of the fairies," I heard Elsie whisper to her younger cousin. "We need proof!"

"I've seen them and you've seen them," Frances replied. "We know they exist. If only they would stay still, even for a second."

Duh! Of course we exist!

"Until then, we'll have to keep using these cardboard cut-outs."

I crept out of my acorn shell in time to see Elsie pinning a picture of someone who looked exactly like me on to *my* toadstool.

"Sir Arthur Conan Doyle is coming over tomorrow, and he'll detect that our photographs are fake!" Frances said.

"Kneel down and smile at it and pretend it's real," Elsie said. "Say cheese!"

There was a loud flash, worse than the lightning strike that hit our oak library five winters ago, and I raced back into my acorn shell.

*

Dawn fairy was just setting out her pearly knives when Elsie, Frances and a man with a moustache, pipe and a butterfly net turned up on our daisy step.

Queen Titania rustled her wings for silence in the beech trunk hallway. "Remember, we have melted into the shadows for centuries and that is how we've survived. So, what must we do?"

"Melt into the shadows," we all chorused.

Though I felt a bubble of resentment inside.

"Where do you normally see them?" the man with the moustache asked Elsie and Frances.

"Over there," Frances replied and she seemed to point directly at me. Her camera was slung around her neck, and I noticed for the first time that her eyes were the colour of new spring grass.

"Sometimes we have to wait a long time Sir Conan," Elsie added. "Hours even!"

"Really?" Sir Conan said. "I'm not sure if you and your younger cousin aren't just making it up. A little pretend game, eh? To fool us adults?" He picked up his butterfly net. "I don't believe fairies exist."

I felt the stone of rebellion rising up.

Don't exist? Moi? I'll show him!

I jumped out of the beech hall just as Frances held the camera to her eye.

"Cheese!" I yelled and the flash nearly blinded me.

And that, reader, is how the last photograph of the Cottingley fairies taken by Elsie Wright and Frances Griffiths is considered to be genuine.

Wolf

By Thilda Haylock
Sixteen years old from Meilen, Switzerland

The classic story of The Three Little Pigs retold from the view of the wolf.

Once upon a time, on a bright, sunny morning, I was out walking when suddenly I heard voices. "Take care, my dears, and remember to watch out for the big bad wolf, for he is very dangerous."

Oh, they're talking about me, I thought to myself. I crept closer and then climbed a tree to listen.

"Yes Mummy!" answered three voices. "Don't worry about us."

Through the thick branches, I spied three little pigs. They were happily walking along the path, baskets of food in hand. I waited a minute and then I jumped down and started to follow them, curious as to where they could be off to so early in the morning.

After a while, the little pigs came across a man with a big bundle of straw.

"Oooh!" said the first little pig. "This will make a fantastic house! What do you think, my dear brother and sister?"

"Well," said the second little pig. "I think that it will be a bit unstable."

"I agree," said the third little pig. "We're going to keep looking."

"Suit yourselves," said the first little pig. He rolled and bought the bundle of straw from the man. The other two pigs kept walking.

Now, me being me, I always want what's easiest. I was also already quite tired and so instead of following the other pigs, I hid in the bundle of straw, while the first little pig started to build his house. It didn't take long, and by lunchtime he had already finished. The little pig settled down and started to eat his lunch.

I was starting to get hungry so I walked up to the house, knocked on the door and shouted, "Little Pig, it's the Big Bad Wolf. Let me in!"

"And if I don't?" replied a scared little voice.

I tried to think, but I could never think very clearly when I was hungry, so I said, "Then I'll huff and I'll puff and I'll blow your house down."

"I won't let you in!" said the first little pig. "My mother told me you're very dangerous!"

I hated to do it, but I never go back on my word and so I huffed and puffed and then I blew with all my might. Straw flew everywhere. I looked for the little pig, but he had disappeared.

I sat down, wondering what to do next. *Perhaps I should try to find the other little pigs?* I got up and continued in the direction that I last saw them heading towards. Before long I reached a house made of sticks. I peered through one of the windows and there sat the second little pig with her brother next to him.

I knocked on the window and once again called out, "Little pigs, little pigs, let me in!"

The little pigs looked at me in horror and the second little pig shouted, "And if we don't?"

Exasperated, I shouted back, "Then I'll huff and I'll puff and I'll blow your house down!"

I was getting tired of this game.

The little pigs looked at each other and answered, "We won't let you in!"

And so I huffed and I puffed and I blew the stupid house down. Sticks went flying everywhere and by the time it had settled the little pigs were nowhere to be seen.

I laid down under a nearby tree, which seemed to have lost all its leaves, and stared sadly into the distance. The sun was now so low in the sky that it looked like a ball of fire, swimming alone in a big ocean and it hit me that I was lonely.

I got up continued along the path. After a while, I reached a very sturdy-looking house made of bricks.

Now that's a very nice house, I thought to myself. I crept up to it and peered through the front window.

There sat the three little pigs talking together, cosy by a warm fire. They looked so happy. I went to the door and knocked. The voices fell silent.

I breathed in and spoke quietly, "Little pigs, little pigs, please let me in."

Just when I thought they wouldn't answer, the shout came, "Go away big bad wolf! Our mother warned us about you. You're dangerous. Go away, because we don't want you here."

Anger started to boil deep within me. *Why couldn't they just let me in?*

"Then . . . then I'll huff and I'll puff and I'll blow your house down!"

"Go away," came the answer once again.

I backed away and then, for the last time, I huffed, then I puffed and I blew for all I was worth. All the anger, pain and rejection that I was feeling went into it. But the house stayed up.

I could hear the pigs laughing so I turned tail and ran, but I didn't go far. I stopped not far from the house and sat down.

I stared up into the sky and did something that I had only ever done once before, when my father was shot by a hunter . . . I cried. You see, after my father's tragedy, I decided that I had enough of everybody's fear. I just wanted to show them that I couldn't help being a wolf. I couldn't help looking like this. I wanted to show these little pigs that there was nothing to be afraid of, but who was I kidding? I'm a wolf. No one was ever going to love me.

Tears fell from my eyes and I howled to the sky. The creak of a door got my attention and then feet pattering across the grass. A shadow fell across me and a gentle voice said, "Are you alright, Big Bad Wolf?"

I looked up and saw the third little pig standing next to me, with the others not far behind and that's when I realised that sometimes, to show someone who you really are, you need to be vulnerable. Barging up and threatening to blow down their house was never going to get me anywhere.

"And we ended up being quite good friends didn't we, little pigs?" I asked from my chair in the little pigs' house.

"Yes, we did," the third little pig said. "But come on, Wolf, enough story time. Let's go and have some dinner, because I'm starving."

The Wolf Prince of Insopia Grove

By Haley Fisher
Seventeen years old from Ontario, Canada

Complete, eternal happiness is when your heart beats a little faster and boiling blood flows rapidly through your veins. The world gleams as if it obtained a blissful hue of ecstasy. Every stride along your path is taken with confidence and passion. The sweet, aromatic scent of mother's freshly baked cookies forever lingers in the air with the comforting presence of high spirits prancing about.

The sun shines brighter, and a rainbow lines the sky. Your favourite joyous tunes are set on repeat. Every single one of your heart's desires is fulfilled within an instant. No need for shooting stars, wishing wells, or magic spells. Everything you could possibly dream of is yours for the taking, including heaven's bells.

One may say this feeling is unachievable and irrational. Every individual is broken in some shape or form. However, light will always fill the cracks, as long as you take the time to notice and appreciate it. Living creatures are driven by one universal emotion that causes us to fight—greed. Greed for power consumes a soul, devouring every last smile, laugh, or tender touch in sight.

Light comes in the form of a certain individual; someone who will be worth living for. Who will chase away the horrors hiding in the dark, slay your demons from your torturous past, or possibly, slay the demon within you. When you look into their hopeful eyes, you know that death is no longer an option. You promise on your heart, body and soul that you will never leave their post. They may be someone you'd sacrifice every last desire for because their presence and smile will be what you long for the most.

True pain is when you lose the one you loved the most, at the fault of your own bloody hands. The preposterous horror you feel when you see the wonder in their eyes fade. The echoing screams and thumps of their limp body hitting the floor, the blood puddle at your feet, in an array of splatter. Your heart abruptly stops just like your lover's, but somehow you stay alive. You breathe in but you cannot exhale. Your blood runs cold, and you wish you were dead. But tragic, doomed fate awaits you instead.

One freezing, autumn night, the wind shrieked through the evergreen trees. The blood moon hovered up above, wreaking havoc on the small village of Insopia Grove. Rain poured from the cloud's fearful eyes; thunder crashed louder than the drums of war.

Missy Bellville, the twelve-year-old princess and future Queen of Insopia Grove, sprinted through the forest. Her drenched, blonde hair spilled out of her dark green cloak. It was a sad attempt to hide what the hungry predator craved. Missy's face was damp, and tears leaked from her crystal blue eyes. Her pale skin was flushed red, as she stopped to catch her breath. She gasped when she heard the low rumble of a growl against her neck.

"Missy Belville, come with me or your kingdom will meet its dreadful demise."

The warm breath against her frostbitten flesh soothed Missy, but the solemn words caused her to shriek in gruesome horror.

I heard her troubled cries from miles away and raced to her side. My brother, in wolf form, stood tall and mighty, teeth clenched together, forming a horrific snarl. As soon as he saw me, he pounced, his body slamming me to the ground.

Missy stood in disbelief, watching two large, dark-coated wolves rip through each other's flesh and fur.

I softly mumbled under my breath, "Missy run."

But she remained still in shock. She always was a curious child, but if she wasn't careful that could lead to her death.

Frustrated and concerned for the girl's safety, I turned around to face her, and howled as loud as I possibly could, urging her to take off like a frightened fawn. Instead, she pulled out a sword her father had given her for protection and swung it at my brother, who had been preparing for another attack.

My brother took a hard blow, as the blade sliced through his right eyebrow above his chocolate-coloured eyes, stunning him. With a whimper, he hit the floor with a loud thump.

Missy stood and watched as if she was waiting for something magical to happen. I howled once again to try to send her off screaming towards her castle. My forest green eyes met hers, begging her to run before the rest of my pack arrived, but it was too late.

Dark-coated wolves slowly stalked towards us, surrounding her with their drool-covered snouts. Yellow, beady eyes watched as her breath quickened, waiting for the right moment to strike. Her delightful scent of vanilla perfume and cherry lip gloss wafted in the damp, cool air.

My brother, in an attempt to save Missy from our hungry relatives, jumped on top of her fragile, mortal body. Her head slammed into the sharp point of a rock, fracturing her skull. Blood splattered everywhere; she would have died. I panicked. I had no choice. I bit into her neck, giving her the bite of a werewolf.

I grabbed her by the hood of her cloak, jumping over my brothers and sisters. She screamed, as my paws ran as fast as I ever thought they could. Her arms and legs scraped against the cold, hard ground, leaving cuts, scrapes and bruises galore. The scent of her blood was almost too hard to not indulge in. It took every bone in my body to refrain my teeth from engulfing her right then and there.

I left her a shivering, sobbing mess on the castle doorstep, and howled at the top of my lungs, hoping to wake the King and Queen of their slumber. The lights immediately switched on, casting an illuminating glow upon Missy's crippled body. That was the night I promised I would never let Missy go through such trauma again. With overpowering sorrow, I quickly scampered back into the forest where beasts like me belong.

In the distance, I heard Missy's parents question her whereabouts.

Missy's voice quivered as she said, "I went to play with my friends Xavier and Damion."

From that night on, the forest was deemed dangerous and the whole town developed into a panicked frenzy. The werewolf bite on the princess' neck caused the King and Queen to barricade the town from the forest; but little did they know that the two monsters they feared were already inside the kingdom, living amongst them as neighbours, friends and shopkeepers.

My brother and I were playing in the village after school when the barricade went up. My wolf pack was out and about in the forest scavenging for our dinner. A magical force field, lined with a silver coating, was plastered on the walls of the village. It was deadly to a werewolf's touch; no werewolves would be able to get in or out of Insopia Grove.

I heard my mother and father howl for my brother and I, but it was too late; we were officially trapped in the kingdom of Insopia Grove.

My brother and I lived amongst Princess Missy Bellville for a little over a decade. We attended different schools because we were poor orphans, placed on the lowest tier of the kingdom's class hierarchy. We worked on the wheat farm. Every day we worked our fingers to the bone. But when Missy Bellville walked down the cobblestone path, our jaws would drop and our heartbeats would quicken.

"Good day Xavier," Missy sung.

The sound of her angelic voice pronouncing my name would ring through my ears, supplying warmth and sunlight to every cell in my body.

"How do you do this fine afternoon?" I asked while quickly stumbling to my knees, grasping her hand, to place a soft kiss upon her fingertips.

My troublemaker of a brother, Damion, picked her up and spun her around. Her ladylike, pink floral dress spun elegantly, as soft giggles escaped her rose-coloured lips.

"Damion! Put me down now!" she shrieked, as Damion barbarically laughed before placing her down gently on the wheat field.

"Now Missy, you ought to be getting home," I said. "It's nearly dark. What can we do for you?"

She teasingly replied, "It is Princess Missy Bellville to you sir, and I wouldn't mind a fresh loaf of bread to eat on the night before I am wed."

"Wed?" Both Damion and I asked with urgent concern.

Missy grinned and nodded. After Missy left, my brother and I frantically reviewed what Missy had told us. She was to get married to Sam Mercury, the son of the King's nobleman. He was one of the kingdom's top hunters; he shoots to kill and succeeds every time. How could the King and Queen marry their princess off to a man who kills her second identity for pleasure?

"Wow Xavier, there is no way anyone would know that girl is a rabid beast," Damion said laughing.

"Yes, the King and Queen did a marvellous job concealing my mistake," I said solemnly.

Damion looked at me for the first time with pity and compassion. "Xavier, it was not your fault; it was the only way. Her parents should be praising you. You should be engaged to her for your honourable action. I would not have had the guts necessary to do it."

A feeling of comfort washed over me, but I knew there was nothing I could ever do to stop Missy's marriage.

Every blood moon, Missy, Damion and I would be locked together in the dungeon of the kingdom. It took some convincing for the King and Queen to let Damion and I bunk with Missy on those nights, but they did not want to risk the spreading of the werewolf curse throughout the kingdom.

Endless nights of board games got us through, but we hated feeling like we were beasts or killers. In our wolf forms, we still have emotions, but humans believe we lose control of our senses. This is partially true, as we face the longing need for protein; however, it does not need to be human protein like all the myths believe. Dozens of canned raw meats can easily relieve the hunger.

But tonight, something was different. Missy didn't show up. Damion and I paced, anxiously waiting with bated breath. I couldn't help it. I howled as loud as I could. We heard a distressed howl from Missy, and Damion was already out the door.

We picked up Missy's scent and tracked her and her hunter down. To my displeasure, her husband to be, Sam Mercury, was the evil culprit. Missy in wolf form, with white as snow fur, whimpered as the wind of Sam's axe sliced through the air, towards her neck. Damion took immediate action, leaping into the air trampling Sam to the ground. Missy cried as I snuggled up to her, while Damion finished Sam off.

The next morning, Damion and I returned the princess back to her castle.

Enraged, I yelled, "What kind of parents are you? You put your daughter in immediate danger and practically disowned her on the night the blood moon hovers above!"

Damion patted my shoulder, urging me to calm myself down, as I was addressing royalty. Her desperate parents practically begged me to marry their daughter in order to supply her with the necessary protection.

Missy, Damion and I smiled in union, excited to make some well needed changes to the kingdom. Werewolves and mortals would soon live in perfect harmony.

Hidden Smiles

By Caitlin Beardsworth
Sixteen years old from Blackburn, England

We never used to be this way. Once upon a time we were . . . something else. Not quite lovers—yet not quite friends either. Friends don't look at each other the way I look at him, or the way he looked at me.

I wish fate would've been different for us. I wish it would've turned out like one of my endless daydreams—him holding me close enough that I can feel his breath ghosting along my neck or with him staring at me from the end of the aisle with laughter in his eyes and a smile on his face. Instead, he's staring down at me with a sneer cruel, twisting his lips, with hate dancing through his eyes. When did we get this way?

Tears filled my eyes and I blinked them away with fierce determination. He already had the satisfaction of breaking my heart. I keep my head bowed and stared resolutely at the cracked grey stone beneath his feet. I was aware that this position made me seem weak, submissive. Despite this I'd rather appear submissive than stare at him.

It was a beautiful spring day. The grass shimmered like emeralds and flowers were in full bloom. The beauty of the palace gardens didn't hold a candle to his ethereal beauty. He looked like a god. Streaks of sunbeams shone through his curls, making his beautiful golden locks glow like an angels halo. His lips were curved into a soft smile that was reserved only for me. How could I not fall in love with him?

I blurted out the truth I had carefully kept hidden for years, too caught up to think about the disastrous consequences. His smile froze and something vulnerable flashed through his eyes. It was gone as quickly as it came and was replaced with a guarded look. He avoided my eyes as he stepped away. In that moment I felt like Icarus. I had flown too close to the sun.

I'm snapped back to the present by the sound of his laugh and for a moment I swear I could see the hate clear in his eyes, but it's only for a moment. I quickly looked away.

"It has come to my attention," he said in a careful, even tone as if he was discussing the weather. "That you have been plotting against me."

I remained silent, not trusting my voice not to break.

"What do you say in regard to that accusation?"

Again, I didn't speak. Evidently, he already knew exactly what I have been up to—he didn't need me to admit anything. He yanked my chin up roughly.

"Answer me," he growled in a low, dangerous voice.

I had only ever heard that voice once before when his father, the king, had accused me of using his son for money as I was a 'lowly stable boy.' My prince's eyes had become slits of ice and his voice dropped a few octaves, as he hissed angry, defensive words to his father.

"We'll talk about this later," the king said. After looking at me up and down, he sneered and stalked off.

My prince had turned to me with apologetic eyes before babbling apologies. I reassured him that it was okay; after all, he wouldn't be the first to assume that. He had nodded with a sigh before engaging me in a conversation about something else, yet it didn't manage to distract me from the way his eyes danced nervously to the direction his father had stalked off to. I brushed it off however when he shot me a dazzling smile, I wish I hadn't.

"I would say that the accusation is true," I admitted.

His hand was still on my chin and his touch made my cheeks flush.

"Why?" he whispered, barely loud enough for me to hear.

I glanced away, unable to hold his gaze, as I whispered back, just as quietly, "I couldn't let you ruin this kingdom in a desperate attempt to please your father."

I heard a sharp intake of breath. His eyes were wide and his lips were parted in shock. He looked so lost that I felt the urge to wrap my arms around him while whispering promises to keep him safe. But I didn't. Instead, I turned my gaze back to the stones beneath our feet. His hand was still on my face and his touch was burning and oh so intoxicating.

Finally, after what seemed like an eternity, he moved his hand away shakily. He took a stuttering breath before facing the court.

"The traitor has admitted to treason. I sentence him to death."

He walked away from me as arms come around my waist and I was dragged away. I screamed his name, his title, his childhood nickname. The last one made him pause for a fleeting moment, before he carried on as though he hadn't hear me. I desperately tried to make him understand that I never plotted anything on his life, merely his court. Yet he never turned back around.

He had once admitted to me, back when we were young and bright eyed, that he would never use the death penalty. We were curled up together giggling as we told each other secrets.

He had gone quiet for a few minutes before murmuring, "I don't want to kill anyone. I just—it seems—I don't want . . ." He took a few breaths in an attempt to calm himself. "I just don't want to be the reason why a family goes without their sister, mother, father, brother. Whoever it is, I don't want to be the reason why their lives are ruined forever."

My heart lurched and I rushed to reassure him that he would never do such a thing; he's too good, too kind, too humane. Seems like time can taint even the sweetest of things.

They threw me in a dark dungeon carelessly, as though I were a rag doll. My head smacked against the floor and I groaned as black spots danced through my vision. The guards laughed cruelly before slamming the door. I sighed and stared at the grime on the ceiling. I don't know how long I stayed there, staring at the ceiling, while a million thoughts ran through my head.

Eventually, the door unlocked and the room was suddenly bathed in light. A silhouette stood at the door. I blinked and sat up as the figure gracefully walked towards me.

I stared up at the figure, feeling an odd mix of desperation, relief, resignation, fear and hope. The only sounds were the sound of our quiet breaths.

"Get up," he said quietly.

I scrambled to comply, apologies fell from my lips and tears appeared in my eyes. He held up a hand and my babbling stopped.

"I should be the one apologising to you—and the kingdom I suppose—for the terrible job I've done at ruling. However, considering you're my entire world I think I'll just apologise to you at the moment."

I remained silent.

"I should not have rejected you so harshly. I admit I was scared. My father ..." His shakes his head and his blonde curls fell into his face. "I made a choice between you and my father. It was the wrong choice. I didn't want to admit I loved you. Love you. It was so hard not to though. With your black curls and whisky coloured eyes. Your dazzling crooked grin and warm laugh. I was too scared of ruining my father's life that I completely disregarded my own. I don't ... I don't know if you could ever forgive me ... I know I don't deserve it. But believe me I will try everything to make it up to you. I love you and I ..."

I cut him off quickly, throwing my arms around him and sealing our mouths in a passionate kiss. I smiled softly against his lips and whispered, "I forgive you."

He reared back before murmuring, "You shouldn't."

"It's mine to give. Let me forgive you."

He stared at me a moment, an unreadable look in his eyes before nodding. I grinned before realising that we were still in the dungeons.

"So, are we getting out of here? Or are we waiting until the guards come to execute me, so we can perform a tragic Romeo and Juliet-style romance?"

He rolled his eyes, a mischievous grin on his face, "Well, we could stay here, if it's your thing. Or you could run away with me and we can start again?"

He looked so hopeful and vulnerable in a way that made my knees weak.

I pretended to think about it, before I smiled and pressed a soft kiss to the corner of his mouth.

"Well, where you go I go, my love, so by all means lead the way."

He beamed and it was so beautiful and warm that I wanted to keep the expression on his face forever. We quietly snuck through the dungeons before we made our way to the stables. I looked around fondly, memories weaving through my mind.

"We'll make new memories," he said, handing me the reigns to a horse.

I smiled and mounted the horse before I rode into the sunset with my happily ever after.

Black and White

By Valerie Anireto
Thirteen years old from Abuja, Nigeria

The sand was softly golden with just the right amount of warmth. The forever stretching sea was masked with an apricot colour, the beautiful umber flowing into turquoise. From the upper left the gulls cried, circling until the fishing fleet returned. The air had that salty, seaweed smell she could still remember nearly fifteen years later.

Little Tammy toddled around in the sand, her pale fingers clutching at anything she could find, from grey dusty pebbles to colourful pink seashells. Ria stood with her arms folded, shivering uncontrollably in her red tank top, as the wind blew through her hair with powerful passion, scattering the locks like leaves in the fall.

Ria felt the golden yellow grains of sand under her feet, watched clouds chasing themselves across the sky, until she saw something: a silver-like metal, twinkling under the gaze of the sky. Her eyes followed the object until she came across it laying on the sand crusted over next to a patch of drying seaweed. It was a necklace.

She picked it up; eyes scrutinising. It had jade stones, the biggest carved into the image of a small dolphin. The necklace awakened memories long forgotten, like the ebbing tide, echoes of the past jarring her mind as a lone tear escaped and trailed down her cheek.

Ria was Black and he was white. They were from two different cultures but with an unbreakable bond. They'd grown up together. Her mother had been his family's household maid, so they got to be around each other a lot. Oh, how she wished to return to those meadows, among the trees which had been planted a long time ago; where she frolicked about the vast plains of the open country. If she thought long and hard enough, she could still remember her mother's forlorn apron, stitched this way and that with all its colourful designs, from teapots to palace guards. She could smell the aroma of freshly baked scones straight from the oven.

Ria could recall the serenity of that world, her world. There was that crackle that came from the *Morning Time* newspaper, the whistle from the old, blackened kettle, the swish from her skirts when she ran under the bright, blue sky as Damien rushed to keep up with her.

Ria once had long, thin legs; now they were thicker with the stress of adulthood. She had been extremely pretty back then, with an undeniable symmetry to her features, her body lithe and athletic, without abundant curves. Her figure hadn't mattered then, but the darkness of her skin had.

Ria remembered fleeting moments when someone staring would inadvertently catch her eye and then hurriedly look away. Their faces were etched with distaste, as if it was her fault they felt offended and annoyed. All because she had brown skin and an inky, black Afro.

It was Damien who taught her to love herself. That beautiful couldn't be described by those starving adolescents they put on magazines—faces that looked so pale and gaunt. Inner beauty wasn't about being anaemic and frail and gangly. He taught her that true beauty was all about simplicity and a tenderness of the soul.

Damien was a white boy with brown hair and eyes of mischief but a heart of gold. His smile was the purest she'd ever seen, for it extended to his eyes and deep into his soul. The way his lips lifted upwards and his one dimple dented his cheek. His teeth were perfectly aligned. She missed all these, but most of all; she missed him.

"Mama."

She summoned up strength from deep inside her very being; her hands trembled with fear and sadness as she wiped away the pain and grime from her face. She slowly stood up.

"It will be okay. Mama's here," she said as she enveloped Tammy in a warm hug.

Her home was the scent of lavender, the delicate blooms placed in one of her mother's old jam jars. The perfume brought out the exquisite purple hue of the walls, the very same shade of spring forget-me-nots in the morning. It was furnished with everything rustic, new paintings daubed on perfect squares of canvas. She collapsed on a mahogany wooden chair, pulling her daughter into the embrace of her arms; her big brown eyes retelling more than just a story.

It had been summertime in Oxford. The month of clear blue skies and colourful plants and shrubs. The air glistened with multicoloured kites; all trying to overtake one another.

It was also the month of freedom, for Ria could go where she pleased, head held high, wearing denim overalls and shorts just like everyone else.

Even as a child, Ria never really had any friends. They either bullied her, called her names, or mocked her. She remembered once when they had all gone straight for her; pummelling, hitting, kicking, biting. Her left eye had become swollen, her face a bloody mess. The shadows of the beating were still on Ria's skin and on her heart. Something that would remain long after her skin and bone disintegrated.

In all the years of her existence, in the many things she had seen, she had come to realise that loneliness was her only dependable friend, except Damien. He was the only friend she'd ever had, who stood beside her. She could remember the days when tears would flow unchecked down her cheeks, the magnitude of her pain to wail or cry out overwhelming, only because she was born with her father's skin. All those years she was taught to be strong, she had to be. But the look on his face brought the tears back like water from a dam, her walls she'd built up collapsed. She'd let him rock her slowly as he comforted her, her tears soaking his chest. He had pulled her back, wiped her tears away with his sleeves, and stared her in the face.

"I got this for you," he said, pulling out the jade dolphin necklace. The very same one she had picked up on the beach. "So you can always remember that you are loved and you don't need to be like them to be happy. You're perfect just the way you are."

Ria had wrapped him in a warm embrace, pulling him close. She never wanted to leave. She felt as if in his arms all her pain had gone away, especially the depression. If only she could stay in his arms forever, safe from the world's harmful people.

"I want you to promise me that you'd never pull the necklace off, as long as you live," he said.

She mumbled, "Yes."

If only she had known she would never set eyes on him again. For Damien was dead. She buried her head into her daughter's hair, mourning the death of the only friend she had ever known.

Moss-laden marble pillars stood as despairing guards on either side of the cemetery threshold. Behind the wrought iron gates were rows upon rows of crumbling gravestone, like the sea of the dead. Porous trees hunched over most of the void spared by the sickening expanse, plunging the rest in shadow. The place echoed mournfully and deathly. As the wind blew across the graveyard harshly, a number of wooden crosses fell off. The smell of old stone filled the dry air and Ria pulled her skirts close to her, eyes searching for Damien's grave.

She found it. His name had been carefully unscripted on a white tombstone, and she knelt down, slowly placing a red orchid on the brown dirt. She could hear the subtle sound of feet, and out of the shadows a tall figure emerged. His skin was as pale as the moon and his features flawless. He smiled; she could never miss that smile anywhere. Damien.

She stood, eyes wide, fingers covering her mouth to prevent her from screaming out loud.

"Why aren't you dead?" she whispered and Damien took a step closer towards her.

"Because I'm a vampire."

The Burglary

By Matthew Wong
Eleven years old from North Point, Hong Kong

Every night Andrew woke up to the slightest noise but this time he woke up at midnight to the soft purring sound of a petrol engine. Andrew groaned quietly and rolled off his bed to peek out of the windows.

As he rubbed his sleepy eyes and focused his vision, he noticed that at least half of the street lamps were off. Andrew thought it was because of a malfunction, however he did notice a minivan parked just a few houses up the street.

Andrew threw open his windows and stuck his head out of the window to get a clearer view. Although it was dark he managed to make out a few burly people climbing out of the minivan. He couldn't help but think that these people looked like thugs from an action film.

Andrew lived in a quiet neighbourhood, so a minivan parked at midnight with people climbing out of was a bit strange. Even though he didn't know what was going on, there were butterflies in his stomach. His instinct told him that these people were up to no good but his parents were on a business trip and wouldn't return until tomorrow.

Andrew quickly woke up his older brother Anthony.

"Why are you awake in the middle of the night and waking me up?" Anthony complained.

"Look outside and you'll see a bunch of thugs up to something," Andrew replied.

Anthony assumed that this was some sort of joke but reluctantly dragged himself to the windows and was shocked by what he saw. Four strangers were heading towards their house.

"Close the windows and curtains and I'll go lock the door," Andrew hissed.

The two boys hurriedly closed the curtains and stacked heavy objects in front of their front door to prevent anyone from breaking in. They then barricaded their bedroom door and windows. Andrew peered out of the window but the people were now outside their front door. They had managed to pick the door lock without triggering their home protection system. The heavy objects they had barricaded in front of the door fell noisily to the floor. They were entering their house!

He told his brother whose eyes went wide.

"Okay, keep your ear by the door and listen to what's going on," Anthony instructed.

Several tense minutes passed and they couldn't hear anything but they were horrified to hear the unmistakable sound of someone walking right outside their bedroom door! Andrew made a 'keep silent' gesture at his brother.

Unfortunately, Anthony was a clumsy boy and he tripped over a chair leg. He fell down with a loud thud. They heard yelling but it wasn't in English.

"I heard a few words which sound like the Russian Mr Petrov taught me at school," Anthony commented.

But the brothers didn't need to speak Russian to realise that someone was trying to force open their bedroom door. Anthony suddenly had an idea.

"Do you remember everything from the rock climbing course in outward-bound?" Anthony asked. "Where's your kit?"

Andrew pulled the rock-climbing kit from under his bed. They hadn't touched it since the outward-bound camp a year ago.

"What do we need it for?" Andrew asked once he found the kit.

"We're going to climb down the window," Anthony said and Andrew shook his head.

"Do we have a choice? Now help me move the barriers in front of the window," Anthony replied irritably.

Anthony then ordered Andrew to tie a rope to something sturdy while he put more barriers in front of the door. But when Anthony was getting ready to climb down, there was a giant thud on their bedroom door and one of the hinges on the door came off! Anthony and Andrew scrambled recklessly to grab the rope and climb down.

Climbing down a wall with only a rope and experience from a one-day beginners rock climbing course was likely to be fatal and this didn't help the brothers' nerves as they started their daring climb down. They didn't communicate in case the thugs heard them and more than once a slight gust nearly blew the boys off the rope. But the pair were lucky. After what seemed like an eternity they reached the back garden safely.

"I just looked inside and no one's there. Let's sneak in via the back door and call the police," Anthony ordered.

"We should tell the neighbours," Andrew argued.

"Remember we toilet-papered and egged their houses during Halloween. They're going to think we're pranking them or something." Anthony sighed.

They couldn't see the thugs anywhere but they weren't going to take their chances. The boys hid in a storage cupboard under the stairs where they could hear people going up and down the stairs.

"We're going to have to hide here all night," Andrew complained.

"Would you rather they find us and kill us or something? Just shut up for once!" Anthony said.

Just then, they heard a distant voice yelling. Anthony and Andrew were delighted to hear that the voice was speaking English.

"Is everything alright? I saw someone crawl out of the window?" said their fussy old neighbour, Mrs Smith.

Suddenly, she gasped and there was a bang before everything went silent again.

"What did they do to her?" Andrew asked, with his eyes wide.

The stairs above Andrew and Anthony nearly collapsed as the heavy, burly thugs rushed down the stairs. A door slammed and there was silence throughout the house.

"Do you think they've gone?" Andrew whispered but Anthony didn't reply.

Anthony wouldn't admit it but he was too scared to say anything. Andrew bravely opened the storage cupboard's door just a little and saw a deserted sitting room.

"I'm sure they've gone," Andrew said.

"Okay, let's go and see what they have taken from our house," Anthony said.

Andrew came out of the storage cupboard first but screamed in shock when he saw Mrs Smith lying on the doormat, completely still.

"What are you screaming about?" Anthony said as he crawled out of the cupboard.

He froze when he saw Mrs Smith but quickly regained his older-brother-knows-best composure before running over to her. He tried to remember everything he had learnt in a three-week youth first-aid course.

"I think she's breathing!" Anthony declared.

"Is she in some sort of coma?" Andrew asked.

"Hard to say, but I think so. You check if anything is missing and get the phone so I can call an ambulance."

Andrew was pleasantly surprised that nothing was missing. Which made him think what were the thugs looking for? He grabbed the phone and gave it to his brother. Anthony was just about to call 999 when strong hands grabbed his shirt collar from behind.

"All the neighbours warned you that we would get you back for vandalising our houses," Mrs Smith said.

Andrew and Anthony screamed. The door opened and all the neighbours were staring at them and laughing including the strangers that had snuck into their house. They had finally gotten revenge on the devious brothers.

Temptation

By Tommy Bustard
Ten years old from County Antrim, Northern Ireland

One day, a boy called Harry was in his garden playing football when suddenly he kicked the ball too hard and it went over the fence and into his neighbour's backyard. Harry knew that his neighbour was a very weird, old man and he knew that he might not get his ball back. But he wanted to try so he knocked on his neighbour's door but there was no answer. He knocked again. No answer.

Five long minutes later, a tall, dishevelled-looking man came to the door and said, "What do you want boy?"

"I've just come to get my ball back please. It landed in your backyard."

"You may have your ball back if you can do one thing for me."

"Okay," Harry replied. "What would you like me to do?"

"Oh boy, there's one thing I've longed for for five years now and I just can't get it out of my head. I would love a sweet, crunchy, sticky, colourful lollipop."

"Okay," Harry said surprised. "That's easy!"

And off Harry went to get this strange man his sweet, crunchy, sticky, colourful lollipop. Harry ran straight to the local newsagents that he knew had a good selection of sweets.

"Hello Charles," he said to the small, friendly man behind the counter. "I would like a sweet, crunchy, sticky, colourful lollipop please."

"Sorry Harry, but I only have sweet, crunchy, sticky lollipops left. They are not colourful. Will that do?"

"Yes, I'm sure that will be just fine. Thank you Charles."

"You're welcome Harry."

But when Harry gave the sweet, crunchy, sticky lollipop to his neighbour he said, "This will not do. I asked for a sweet, crunchy, sticky, *colourful* lollipop, not a sweet, crunchy, sticky lollipop, you silly boy."

Harry groaned because he knew the other sweet shop was all the way on the other side of town! When Harry arrived at the sweet shop on the other side of town, he walked in and saw a sweet, crunchy, sticky, colourful lollipop on one of the shelves! Harry was so happy to see it. All he had to do now was buy it!

He went up to the shopkeeper and said, "May I have a sweet, crunchy, sticky, colourful lollipop please?"

"Yes, that will be £2 please."

Harry looked in his wallet and . . . he only had £1! He was devastated. He had spent most of his money on the sweet, crunchy, sticky lollipop!

"I will be back in half an hour," Harry said.

Harry could not believe his bad luck; he had been trying for so long just to get his football back. His Mum would be worried. He couldn't even call her because he had left his phone at the house!

After a long, miserable twenty minutes he had the money and he finally brought the sweet, crunchy, sticky, colourful lollipop. As he was walking back on the long, journey home, his stomach rumbled, and he completely forgot about the man and the football.

Ten minutes later there was no sweet, crunchy, sticky, colourful lollipop left.

The Talent Show

By Ana Cuesta
Eleven years old from Valencia, Spain

Peter was in school when he found out about the talent show. Signing up would give you the chance to show off how much talent you had and at the end, the judges would vote. At first, Peter was unsure about signing-up, but he did spend a lot of time thinking about it. The problem was, he did not consider himself to have any true talent. In the end, he registered his name because, surely, he must have at least *one* hidden talent.

He tried painting, basketball, writing and even pottery... nothing. Nothing was quite right. The thing that Peter felt he did worst of all was painting. Every time he tried to paint or draw something, he ended up with a piece of abstract art.

Peter was disappointed in himself because the show was approaching, and he still hadn't discovered any real talent of his own. He was beginning to feel stressed but that evening, as he looked over his artwork, he suddenly had an idea.

When the day finally arrived, the huge auditorium was packed with more people than he could have ever imagined. Teachers, children and parents had all come to see the performances.

During the show he saw many children with different talents. There was one boy who could play the piano with his toes. Whilst the men backstage carried on the big, heavy piano, the young boy removed his shoes and began playing as quickly as possible. Incredible!

One girl was great at gymnastics. Again, the men from backstage appeared, this time carrying a school bag, which they left in the middle of the stage. Unexpectedly, a leg appeared from inside, then another. The judges were very surprised. She could fit perfectly inside the bag.

"Amazing!" they cheered.

Peter knew it was going to be hard to win.

One boy grabbed a pen and pushed it inside his ear only for it appear out the other side. They were all very weird and quite extraordinary talents.

Now it was Peter's turn. He took a piece of paper and drew as badly as he possibly could.

"This is abstract art," he announced. The paper was a mix of colours. "It has a hidden message like a lot of famous abstract paintings and this one is no different. Only the smartest people who know all about art could possibly understand it. "

The thing Peter realised is people want to think they are smart, so unsurprisingly they all voted for him and he won!

Peter won not because he had a weird and quite extraordinary talent but because he was smart and that differentiated him from all the other kids on the stage.

Beetle-Weetle: What a Day

By *Niall Hamilton-Ellis*
Six years old from Doncaster, England

One morning, Beetle-Weetle woke up and decided that he would like a bowl of spiders for breakfast. He went downstairs in his tree house, poured the spiders into his bowl and went to the fridge to get some milk for his breakfast. But when he arrived at the fridge, he could not find the milk!

"What a day!" Beetle-Weetle sighed.

Beetle-Weetle really wanted spiders for breakfast, so he set off to the shop for some milk. A short time later he arrived and picked up the milk and took it to the till to pay.

"That'll be £1 please," the shop keeper said.

"Oh no, I've forgotten my wallet!" Beetle-Weetle cried. "I need to go home to get it. What a day!"

Beetle-Weetle was rushing so much to get home that he didn't see the giant puddle in his path.

SPLASH!

Beetle-Weetle landed face first in the huge puddle!

"What a day!" Beetle-Weetle sighed.

Wet and annoyed, he continued on his journey home, when he was spotted by a nearby bird who wanted

Beetle-Weetle for her breakfast! He dashed for the nearest bush and jumped inside, safe from the bird.

"What a day!" Beetle-Weetle sighed.

As Beetle-Weetle stood up from his hiding place, he smelled something funny. He had been so desperate to hide from the bird that he hadn't seen what the bush had been covering. Stinky, smelly dog poo! And it was all over Beetle-Weetle's bottom.

"What a day!" Beetle-Weetle sighed.

Finally, Beetle-Weetle arrived home.

"Safe at last, I'd better go get clean."

After a long, warm shower Beetle-Weetle was thirsty.

"I think I'll have some juice before I go back to the shop," he said to himself.

Beetle-Weetle opened the fridge, reached in, grabbed the juice and what was behind it? The milk!

Beetle-Weetle laughed, as he finally munched on his bowl of spiders.

The Journey Across London

By Jacinta Khadouri
Eleven years old from London, England

Slowly walking along the busy high street as the morning light stroked the trees and glistened on the damp leaves, a little girl was clutching tightly to her big, blue balloon. Suddenly, a gust of raging wind came out of nowhere, sweeping the balloon out of the small girl's fingers.

Frantically, she chased the balloon, but it only flew higher and higher, until she lost sight of it among the varying cotton wool clouds in the dazzling blue sky. She cried inconsolably but the balloon was free.

Gliding carefree through the air, feeling as if he were a bird, the balloon looked down and saw the colossal bustling city of London. Instantly, he heard a vast range of sounds as joyful children shouted in delight whilst playing their games. Cars zoomed past as fast as lightning on the roads that circled and split the city like strings of spaghetti. Modern glass hotels and dilapidated metal factories were scattered everywhere throughout London.

"There are so many imposing buildings and countless houses. There isn't any nature here. I want to smell the fresh air, not all these toxic fumes," the balloon said to himself.

He felt hopeful about where the wind would carry him. He drifted for hours feeling optimistic and enjoying the views of the rooftops until he saw the meadows.

"Look at all these lush green pastures and colourful bright flowers." The balloon sighed.

He floated over some rolling hills and down into a verdant valley arriving at a trimmed and tidy garden, as the last rays of sun painted the hills.

In the moonlight, he bounced along the manicured lawn bordered symmetrically with pretty flowers and tropical plants barely visible now in the darkness of the night. The first stars lit up the sky as he floated past a pond that was a huge blanket of shimmering silver.

"What beautiful rose bushes there are. I want to smell their lovely scent."

Suddenly, he realised how many thorns they had. Hurriedly, he desperately struggled against the wind's strong current trying to get away from their menacing spikes of death. But it was too late. There was a pop, bang, hisssss . . .

The balloon fell to the ground deflated, only left with his memories of his freedom from the time he was up above.

Anxiety

By Maahum Nazir
Seventeen years old from London, England

All I could think of were the deadlines, both near and distant. All I wanted to do was to drift into the world of dreams. All I desired was for the inkiness of my brain to be relieved.

Yet, my brain was a washing machine—a violent whirl of chaos. The fear of falling into a pit of disappointment and despair was overwhelming. The pressure and the stress wrapped around me like a child's blanket. Only it suffocated me. Suffocated any desire to move, think or live.

I was sitting alone. There was no love; no home; it was an aura of agitation. It was raining, but I was glad. The pitter patter of the rain seemed to create a shield around me. Trying to protect me from my unfortunate fate; or at least the unfortunate fate I thought I was deemed.

The clouds clustered together. It silently loomed over my bedroom window as it shadowed every bit of sunlight. The inkiness of my brain was showing its presence in front of my eyes. The thunder was cracking the air; as if heavens would split apart. It was rolling like the ash of a volcano, morphing into a rolling, booming rumble. It was my saviour—violent, uncontrollable and turbulent, yet it soothed, appeased and calmed my anxiety.

I desperately needed to calm down. I looked up into the night sky. It was like when star gazing, everything becomes so big, glorious and overwhelming and I became the microscopic being, the insignificant, shivering wreck.

My heart continued to race and all I wanted to do was to curl up into a ball. I wished I could sit inside that very washing machine, in the corner of the basement where all the stress, anxiety and weight would be lifted off my shoulders—spinning, tumbling and washing away all the inkiness of my brain, which fazed me restlessly.

In an attempt to clear my mind, I walked down into my basement. It was the only source of comfort, as if I had subconsciously found myself folding laundry. I loved to feel the warm cloth, the sense of order, the feeling of accomplishment. It allowed my creativity to run wild. Free to explore ideas and embrace new concepts. There was no room for failure.

I glanced over to the washing machine. The once violent, uncontrollable, turbulent spinning had settled. The ripples of water were smooth as I pressed my nose against the door of the machine. The smoothness of the process and the lack of troubles reflected my mental state. I knew it was deceptive though. A temporary satisfaction that put me into a false sense of security. I could not see behind the water. What torment, horror, and anxiety awaited? It was a constant morphing of emotions. The rapid tumbling of the machine would instil the fear so that my guts were tortured yet the lack of movement of the machine lulled me into a false security.

My attention was diverted to the pile of clothes that lay crumpled waiting to be folded. In fact, my eyes pierced into the crisp white blouse that lay on top of the stack full of crumpled clothes. The white blouse that I was destined to wear and had worn every time. White reflected when I was weightless of burdens, my mind filled with light. Only because there is nothing in it.

The inkiness of my brain does not even find me worthy. I know that like a rabbit in headlights, fear of failure would continue to engulf my conscience.

I tenderly graze the sleeves and begin to fold, one arm at a time. The blouse dropped on to the folded pile, giving a sigh of content. The order of the process, the repetitive nature of the same skill found me in my comfort zone. The freshly washed laundry, pungent of lavender, immersed me into ignorant bliss.

Once again, the machine in the corner of the room erupted into a pandemonium, violently throwing a mesh of grey and white clothes against each other and the pounding filled my head.

The Storm in the Glass

By Poppy Dawid
Fourteen years old from London, England

I sometimes hear whispers, endless streams of voices, rushing and reverberating through my head. They come and go—the whispers. Some days, I can hardly hear them at all. They're simply another background noise, like the sound of every inhale and exhale, like the trickle coming from the stream outside my window. Most days, I can hear them well enough to make out every single word but I can still block them out if I try hard enough.

But then come the times when the ever-so-persistent murmurs grow to a crescendo in my ears. The times when everything's hissing and screeching, racing and whirling and rattling through my head, bashing on anything, on everything that can be found in a vain attempt to be let out—

Just like the storm in Ma's crystal.

No, I mentally scold myself. I can't go there again, be it mentally or otherwise. I can't risk what could've happened last time. What almost did happen last time.

"*. . . be careful.*"

Snippets from the past join the voices in my head.

"*. . . moving towards me.*"

No matter how hard I try to keep them from infiltrating my mind, the memories just keep on flowing, taunting me, showing me how close I was to plunging the whole world into chaos.

"*. . . you were lucky this time.*"

And yet there's still a part of me that longs to know what happened. That wants to go back to see that storm in that glass just one more time. Because if I don't know what happened, how can I stop it from happening again?

Every single night, the same questions haunt me—how did it happen? Why? What if it happens again? In the day, it's the fact that the storm-crystal is so close, yet so far out of my reach. I'm stuck in a loop, trapped inside the thought that whatever I choose to do will be wrong.

Tonight is no different. My mind buzzes with what-ifs while my body refuses to move, and I know I can't keep up this cycle forever. Some things only change when you force them and this is one of them. And it will change.

I force myself to sit up, telling myself that if I decide to go, I would be going down there to prevent the crystal shattering. I'll be going for all the right reasons and yet I still can't stop the guilt from eating away at my insides. Because maybe I'm not going for the reasons I say I am.

Maybe, deep down, I know I'm still as entranced by the idea of complete and utter chaos encased within glass, as I was two years ago. Because I know I want to reach out and see what the storm really feels like.

Almost as if sensing my thoughts, my mind is consumed by the voices. I hear them screech, "*Let us out and let the world be free.*"

And suddenly a thought comes into my head that, momentarily, displaces all my doubts. The crystal might be able to let the voices out. It might be able to let them out of my head.

I stand up and put one foot forward. It's only my first step, and I already feel the doubts returning. But free is good, isn't it? I sneak a look at Ma's bedroom before turning away. A small sigh almost escapes my lips before I catch it in my throat. I can't tell her.

What would I even say? That I, her only daughter, hears voices in her head? That she's drawn to the forces of chaos, to the very things that her family's promised to restrain? Ma wouldn't even believe me and perhaps that's a good thing. I steel myself as I continue walking. These sorts of things are best done alone.

As soon as I see it, I can think of nothing else. Even the voices seem to be mumbling through cotton wool, gradually becoming silent, as all my senses focus on the crystal before me.

I take a step forward. It's beautiful. From my position, I can see it all so perfectly—the way the smooth, clear sphere of glass seems to reflect every little pinprick of light that reaches its surface, as if forming a shape, a timeless piece of art. Nothing is eternal, but it seems like every single enchanting moment lasts forever.

Another step.

I realise how foolish I was to even assume it was a sphere—how can I have ever thought it to resemble something so common? In the place of what used to be an artefact of chaos now stands an elegant, exquisite, perfect crystalline structure; a diamond, glittering with the rays of a thousand suns.

Just one more step.

As I peer past the surface and into the realms of chaos that lie beneath, I see that even the storm is beautiful in a way. I watch how it moves around its vessel in a dazzling, unpredictable dance and I wonder why anyone ever thought it had to be sealed away. Everybody must have been senseless.

I'm close enough that I can touch it, and I do exactly that. My hand reaches through the air, fingertips straightening as my heart seems to stop. My arm keeps moving forward as I feel my fingertips finally brush against the glass.

Time seems to pause for a second as a feeling of pure bliss takes over. But everything comes crashing back down again, as I see a crack exactly the same size and shape as it was two years ago. A crack that breaks me out of my trance, but this time, there's nobody to keep it sealed. This time, I can't keep the crevices from creeping over the once-clear surface.

I stare down at the orb, seeing it for the first time for what it truly is. All beauty gone, my eyes widen in horror as I see nothing more than a simple ball of glass containing a never-ending storm of disorder. A ball of glass, containing chaos itself that I've broken.

The last thing I remember before everything shatters is feeling as if I had plunged into Arctic waters, as I realise that it was never my head they wanted to escape. It was always about the crystal but it's too late for me to do anything. The glass has fractured too much and the ice in my chest can't freeze the storm.

I feel weightless and still, suspended in a state of something that's not quite life, but not exactly death. I feel eternal.

I am eternal.

But I had thought that about the crystal. The crystal! The thought hits me like a sudden wind—the only thing even remotely close to movement in this plane of stillness. What happened to it? And where am I? I know nothing about this realm, nothing apart from the eerie silence and the unsettling peace—even the familiar voices are soundless.

I don't like this feeling of serenity, because I know everything's not okay. The peace feels too forced. It reminds me of the saying—

I pale or perhaps I don't. I'm not even sure my body exists, not in this strange world. But the feeling of dread is hard to ignore. The calm before the storm and almost at once, everything comes rushing back.

It shattered. That's what happened. The crystal shattered and I feel the world around me move as I'm swept up in what seems to be a harsh, unforgiving torrent of wind. A cyclone carrying me back to my own realm, back to reality, to normalcy. Except it's not normal. I can't even see past the murky gales that surround me. My ears feel like bursting as I hear the voices returning, but they're not whispers instead it's wails, screeches, cackles and they're coming from whatever the world's become outside.

I see something in the gale and try to duck at what I think is an incoming piece of shrapnel, but my body won't obey me. I stand motionless, against my will, as the shard of glass is reflected off an invisible shield that seems to surround me, protect me. But is it really protecting me from outside forces? Or restraining me from the rest of the world?

I focus with whatever I have to close my eyes, to distract me from everything happening around me, but even that doesn't work. With my eyes shut, I still somehow see myself; everything is clear, directly projected into my mind's eye.

I'm at the eye of the storm. I am the eye of the storm. My hair flails wildly around me as I seem to float, eyes completely white, my mouth wide open in a silent scream. I'm controlling the storm, but the storm is controlling me. I'm so powerful but powerless at the same time.

And I'm scared. But even that's draining away.

Out of the corner of my vision, I see a shape scurrying through my storm, trying to take something. I open my eyes. It's somebody I know, but I can't recognise them. As I gaze upon what might have been an important figure in my life, I can only feel hatred, a sliver of order disrupting this beautiful chaos.

I snarl as it begins to chant; snarl as it starts to call something from my storm. Rage clouds my vision and everything flickers red as all my thoughts scream.

How dare it try and disturb my divine chaos? How dare it try and disturb me?

By the time I realise what's really happening, nothing can be done. My open mouth makes a sound for the first time as I scream, the cry shaking the foundations of the entire world. I howl and shriek as the broken glass rushes towards me, encircles me, tears the forces of chaos from my head. In a desperate endeavour to keep a hold of my storm, my cries grow louder and higher, as I focus everything on tearing apart the intruder, on seizing hold of its feeble body and dragging it back with me. I was not going down alone.

But I watch in rage and horror as the glass seals itself, as my beautiful storm is trapped in its prison once more. I'm left on the floor, chest heaving, sniffling and coughing, grabbing onto whatever I can find to stop the hot tears racing down my cheeks, blindly searching for something, for anything, that might just take everything away.

When I finally calm down, and the tears have stopped streaming and are simply dripping into the floor at a steady pace, I look around for Ma. I want to say so much. I'm sorry and I'd never even risk a glance at the crystal again. I want to tell her thank you, both from me, and from the world.

I look around but she isn't there. The only place I don't glance at is the crystal. Because I refuse to believe what my heart already knows.

That she's in there with the storm in the glass.

About The Lil' Author Skool

The Lil' Author Skool is a not for profit organisation. It was founded in 2016 by award-winning children's author Abiola Bello, who wrote her debut novel *Emily Knight I am . . .* at just aged 12! Because of the writing opportunities she got as a teenager, she wanted to create an exciting competition for young voices from all over the world. The Lil' Author Skool's books are The Originals and Gen Alpha-Z which is available in paperback.

If you would like to enter The little BIG Book Comp, check our website for more details.

Find out more at www.thelilauthorskool.com
Follow on Twitter: @lilauthorskool
Instagram: @thelilauthorskool
Facebook.com/thelilauthorskool

About the Authors
The authors in Daydreamers are:

Nicky Anderson
Valerie Anireto
Katie Bates
Caitlin Beardsworth
Emma Bowler
Tommy Bustard
Ana Cuesta
Poppy Dawid
Honor Dent
Chloe Evans
Haley Fisher
Sejal Gautam
Niall Hamilton-Ellis
Thilda Haylock
Thomas Johnston
Jacinta Khadouri
Nicole Kravstov
Megan Kruger
Amy Lever
Loveday Lock
Maahum Nazir
Maddie Parkhouse
Johana Pusuluri
Emma Uren
Atlas Weyland Eden
Matthew Wong
Andrew Wyles